I0658444

# Gold Lamé

*(that's le-mayy)*

C. Pic Michel

*More information about the writing and*
*artwork of C. Pic Michel can be found at*

**www.cpicmichel.com**

# Gold Lamé

*(that's le-mayy)*

C. Pic Michel

HeartStudio *Books*          Cincinnati, Ohio, USA

With gratitude for JAH who dreams with me.

*Gold Lamé* (that's le-mayy)
*All rights reserved.*
*Copyright © 2008 by C. Pic Michel*
*No part of this publication may be reproduced or transmitted in any form or by any means, electronic or mechanical, including photocopy, recording or by information storage or retrieval system, without permission in writing from the publisher. For information address: The HeartStudio, LLC*

*HeartStudio Books is a registered trade name of The HeartStudio, LLC. in the state of Ohio, USA. E-mail: TheHeartStudio@fuse.net*

PRINTED IN THE UNITED STATES OF AMERICA.

# Contents

Appendix
*Discussion points*

## Explanation of Font Usage

"Text in quotes"
Spoken aloud


*Text in Italics*
"Spoken" in thought
also spoken by Narrator


"Text in *italics* in quotes"
Emphasized aloud


*Pause, pause, pause...*
Narrator channel surfing


Double line space
Slight change, same-scene


## Pronunciation


Hrim — Hreem
Jahni — Johnny
Shima — Sheema
lamé — *that's le-mayy*

# 1

## Shoes, Snails, and Elephants

Amelia Bradford peered over her round knees covered in shimmering taupe colored stockings, and ogled her gold lamé strapped shoes. *Now when did I get those?* She quietly contemplated as the waiter approached the table.

"Have you come to a decision?" The waiter reminded her of Zeke. *It must be something about the eyes*, she thought, and then smiled.

"May I have a few more minutes?" she asked as she glanced down at the menu on the table.

"Ma'am." How she hated hearing the word. "There are people waiting," the waiter smiled, "and you've been sitting here for nearly three hours. Perhaps you could give me a break and do something?" He shrugged, "The manager's getting kinda' hot to move the table."

Amelia followed the jerk of the waiter's head toward the man

1

standing in the far corner of the room. The manager was wearing a black cape and had small horns protruding through the short dark hair on his head. He smirked at Amelia as she noticed he was dangling one blue and one red stiletto heeled shoe by the ankle straps from the fingertips of either hand.

*What the hell is this place?* Amelia thought. "I'm leaving," she told her waiter and started to rise.

"I'm afraid that's not possible." The waiter put his hands on Amelia's shoulders and pressed her back into the booth seat. "You're not in any state to leave." He bent low and looked deeply into her eyes. "The choice is simple ma'am," he continued. "Are you a blue state or a red state?"

"I'm not a state at all!" Amelia's head began to swirl with confusion as she tried to reconcile the manager and his horns, the gold lamé shoes and the political overtones of her dining experience. She heard music, Rumba music. Amelia turned to look over her shoulder as a string of dancers headed toward her table. They wore contorted masks and long dingy blue capes. Each moved in awkward, overly dramatic ways from which Amelia surmised either she or the dancers might be drunk. As they passed her table they chanted, "You're not a state. You're in no state. You're not a state! You're in no state." Feeling her jaw hanging slack Amelia clamped her mouth closed and turned back to the waiter.

"Your chariot awaits." The waiter motioned gently to his side as a long table was rolled in place beside him by two bus boys. Amelia shook her soft reddish curls out of her eyes as she tried to focus.

"Chariot?" she asked.

"It's time to take a little ride," the waiter counted, "One, two, three." Amelia felt herself being lifted into the air and settled again suddenly into place.

"Where am I going?" Amelia struggled to look around from her new angle on the room. Brightly shining lights were temporarily blocked as the round mustached face of Jackie Gleason loomed over her. The shape of his face stretched in and out of focus as if Amelia was viewing him through a fish-eyed lens.

"Don't worry," he said. "Everything is going to be just fine."

"Who are you?" Amelia asked with increased panic in her voice as he turned away, kicked up his heels and dashed away through a set of swinging doors shouting, "And away we go!"

The table on which she was laying was rolling right behind the dancing man. Amelia thought she was going to faint as she watched the walls and overhead lights slide past in a blur. Then she realized she was in fact fainting. She looked around wildly trying to focus on something that would help her maintain consciousness. She wasn't sure where she was, what she had eaten, why the waiter was now rolling her down a long hallway, or what would happen next.

Most of all, she felt absolutely no comfort when Judy Garland appeared next to her shoulder and bent down to whisper in her ear, "People come and go so strangely around here."

*Pause, pause, pause...*

Amelia opened her eyes to find herself surrounded by the brightest white she'd ever seen. Feeling the cool lick of mist on her face she realized she was trying to peer through fog. *Oh thank God. I thought I was heading for the light!* She couldn't see further than a few feet in front of her. Through the silence she could hear the rush of her blood circulating through her ears. *No, my heart is still beating. I'm definitely alive.* A deep need for comfort flooded over her. "Zeke?" she called out as she turned around waiting for a response.

A nudge from behind her right knee pulled Amelia around quickly. The gold lamé heels caught in the ground beneath her and Amelia crumpled to the ground. A wet nose and tongue poked her in the face as she instinctively gathered a wiggling dachshund pup into her arms. "Zeke! Where the hell have you been?" She pushed his wet searching nose aside and pulled his small body closer.

3

Zeke pulled his head back and studied Amelia's face. "I've been snoozing at Sherry and Jill's where you left me against my will, remember?"

"Actually, no," Amelia replied as she marveled at Zeke's deep voice with a Brooklyn accent. Zeke hopped out of Amelia's arms and leaned to one side as he sat on the ground in front of his fallen mistress.

"And where da' hell have you been, missy?"

"What do you mean?" Thoughts of insanity ran through Amelia's mind as it registered that her dog was engaging her in verbal dialogue.

"Well, you didn't come home last night and now you call me into your dream. How long am I going to have to stay in that god forsaken hell hole?"

"Zeke, Sherry and Jill love you," Amelia chided, and then wondered, *They do?* Amelia was unable to pinpoint exactly who Sherry and Jill could be.

"How 'bout telling me where we are?"

"I have no idea." Amelia allowed for the possibility that she could be asleep. "But it doesn't feel like a dream."

"Well, it's not exactly the kinda' dream I'm used to havin' wit' ya', I'll grant you dat." Zeke walked around sniffing into the fog. "I like the dreams where ya' take me for a ride better."

"Well then, aside from the fog, what makes you think I'm dreaming?" Amelia raised herself to an upright position wobbling on the heels beneath her.

"For one thing, you seem to be understanding me pretty good and for another I don't have a Brooklyn accent in *my* dreams." The dog replied matter-of-factly. "Yup, this is mostly, if not entirely your dream."

"I did get you in New York State." Amelia tried to rationalize Zeke's Brooklyn accent as she placed her hands onto her hips trying to stretch away a sharp pain between her shoulders.

"Do we dream together often?" she asked as she tried to peer deeper into the fog.

"Yup." Zeke followed Amelia as she walked around in a circle observing nothing more than white mist. "You dream of me when you're feelin' guilty because you're never home. And I dream you love ta' give me treats." Zeke cocked his head and produced a sad little whiney sound portraying his lonely deservingness of a treat.

Amelia frowned at the chocolate brown dachshund. "You look a little heftier than usual. I must give you too many treats when we're dreaming."

"Never mind me." Zeke changed the subject, "What about 'dose shoes? When da' hell did you get shoes like dat?" Zeke nosed the gold colored leather laces that hugged Amelia's feet.

"I don't know. They just showed up." Amelia took a deep breath and winced as it caught in her shoulders. "I feel stiff." She muttered. "Zeke, how do we get out of here?"

"Can't," Zeke sputtered as he chewed on a barbecued dog treat.

"Hey, I didn't give you that," Amelia protested.

"Yeah you did!" Zeke insisted, "I can dream too!" Amelia sighed as Zeke made more familiar happy dog sounds.

"So why can't we leave?"

"I can. You can't." Zeke gave more information in-between tugging with his teeth at the treat clamped tightly between his paws. "You're having a lucid dream. Well, actually, you're under anesthesia, but it's the next closest thing to lucid dreaming."

"Anesthesia?" Amelia gasped. "Why am I under anesthesia?"

"Because it makes surgery a more comfortable experience?" Zeke sat in front of Amelia and looked up into her hazel brown eyes.

"That's not funny." Amelia's head reeled at the possibility she was having surgery without knowing about it.

"I'm not trying to be funny. It's just the way it is. Stuff happens you know."

"What stuff Zeke? What happened? Why am I having surgery?" Amelia felt her anxiety level rise. She couldn't remember anything

5

being wrong with her.

"I'm not privy to that." Zeke cocked his head. "I got here late. All I know is I was asleep in my pet suite when I heard you calling me so I came running like a good dog." Another barbecued treat appeared on the ground in front of Zeke. "I said 'good dog.'" Zeke repeated, and another treat appeared.

"Enough!" Amelia ordered the treat tally to stop. "You heard me in your sleep?"

"You call me a lot in your dreams, though I don't ever remember you consciously knowing what you were doing once I come running like a good...."

"Stop! Don't you dare!" Amelia eyed Zeke and pointed toward the ground as he flopped into a laying down position. "I'm confused Zeke." Amelia assembled an array of evidence in hopes of finding a clue. "You told me I am under anesthesia then you say you don't know what happened to me because you arrived late. Which is it?"

"In dreams stuff just floats around, Amelia. Info, ideas, other people's dreams. Sometimes it lands in your mind. Other times it bypasses all attempts to get a grip on it. What I didn't know five minutes ago I might know by now. So ask me. What do you want to know?" Zeke looked eager to help while seemingly oblivious to the conversation five minutes earlier.

*What am I doing here?* Amelia shouted in her mind in frustration.

"That's easy," Zeke replied to her thoughts. "You're dreaming and you're awake in your dream."

"But what am I dreaming?" Amelia demanded, "Fog with a dog doesn't seem like much of a dream." Amelia looked up at the fog with renewed confusion in her eyes. *Did you just answer my thoughts?* She looked at the dog.

"It's all thoughts." Zeke replied. "Sound can be out loud or quiet here like a dog whistle. You pick up on it better in dreams. Differently too. More real."

Amelia looked at her little dog turned seeming philosopher. "I can't believe this is happening." She sighed.

"Apparently you do believe it on some level." Zeke countered. "Because it's only about what you believe."

"But I don't want to believe this Zeke. Something's wrong and I don't know what." The dog sat up on his hind legs. "Well, what do you <u>want</u> to do?" he asked playfully trying to make Amelia feel better.

"I want to find out what happened!" Amelia strained to maintain the temper her naturally red curls belied. "Tell me?" she begged her dog.

"Still can't." If dogs could frown Zeke did. Then acting on his hound instinct he added, "But maybe I can help you snoop it out. What's the last thing you remember?" He crouched pushing his hind end up with his tail wagging in the air.

"Judy Garland." Amelia mumbled and stared blankly into the fog.

Zeke's ears went flat as he placed his chin on his paws. He rolled his eyes up at Amelia and let out a soft woof.

"Something tells me we're not in Kansas anymore, Zeke."

*Pause, pause, pause...*

*Snails don't have teeth. The mouth of a snail contains a sort of scraper that it runs along the edge of a leaf to derive the soft juicy tissue. Snails don't have eyes but light receptors at the end of tubules that can lengthen to extend far from the head and retract to nearly disappear inside it. As snails move through their environment their eye tubules wander back and forth examining the surrounding area for food to gnaw upon and water to drink.*

*Resume, resume, resume...*

Jojo Jenkins wasn't surprised when the snail started to move. The snail had been hidden in its shell, attached like a suction cup under the lid of the small plastic terrarium where it lived. Jojo was

7

surprised that he could hear the snail chewing on the leaves he had placed at the bottom of the terrarium. The slow, purposeful activity of the snail had distracted him even more than the Cartoon Network from his summer-school homework.

Jojo watched for minutes as the snail spread wide it's soft, taupe colored body against the side of the clear plastic box. He watched almost breathless as the snail rippled its underside and glided down the side to dip its head in the shallow water dish. His teacher had told him that the snail could live for weeks without coming out of his shell to drink and he must be very patient and keep it in a safe place until he returned to school in the fall. Jojo glanced at the summer math homework in front of him. He didn't feel like he was on vacation, but all the while he watched the snail waking and taking in its environment, he was more peaceful and relaxed than he had been in weeks.

Jojo liked his teacher and the snail that he had named Dumbo. His stepfather had laughed, making fun of the name. "Who names a snail after an elephant? You shoulda' named him Stripe." Jojo's stepfather had pointed his big, rough skinned finger toward the snail. The snail looked tiny compared to the size of the fingertip.

"See that stripe on his back?" Darius Lovell asked in a tone that always made Jojo feel small and insignificant.

"That's his shell," Jojo corrected.

"Whatever." Jojo's stepfather had dismissed the boy as he often did, with a push toward his room. Jojo tended to stay in his room at night just to avoid such encounters with Darius. Once he had his nightly bowl of cereal in hand, everything he needed was in his room.

Jojo looked at the snail as it moved the way his teacher had described, "At the pace of a royal elephant." The day she introduced the snail to the class they also watched the Disney movie Dumbo. At the end of every school session the kids were always too excited about summer break to sit still for very long, so the teacher showed a movie every Friday in May. Jojo identified with Dumbo though he couldn't quite understand that he did.

The baby elephant being separated from his mother gave Jojo familiar feelings. Jojo's mother died when he was a toddler. He had never known his father. After Jojo was born, his mother married his stepfather whom he always called Darius. Darius wasn't very gentle with Jojo. The older he grew, the more Jojo seemed to make Darius angry. They often fought and acted more like brothers than parent and child.

As long as he could remember a caseworker had been present in his life. Every once in a while they would do more than just visit. Once or twice before, Jojo had been removed from the apartment where he lived with Darius. The fight they had at the end of the school year had resulted in their most recent separation. The caseworker gave Jojo a dark green trash bag and asked him to collect some clothes and his pillow. Usually Jojo would listen intently through the crack at his bedroom door to find out what the social worker told Darius he needed to do in order to get Jojo returned to him. This time Darius had been arrested and Jojo felt a strange loneliness for him even though he often wished Darius wouldn't be able to get him back in the past. That night Dumbo kept him company in his new foster home and he comforted himself by remembering he would see his teacher again at the end of the summer.

Jojo dazed off as he watched the snail moving silently across the clear plastic container. He pictured himself holding a feather and flying the way Dumbo the elephant did in the movie. The snail's eye tubules retracted and curved to closely examine the upturned stem of a leaf. It lowered its head and wrapped its mouth around the leaf.

"You're eating a lot." Jojo whispered. "You're going to have a big poop!" Jojo rested his head on the desk in his small room as he fell asleep listening quietly to the snail munching on the leaf.

*Pause, pause, pause...*

9

There was a loud crunch in the fog. Amelia looked down at the ground. Zeke had vanished. The gold lamé shoes remained. She felt panic strike. Amelia stared hard at the fog. Anxious anticipation mounted as if she was the helpless girl quaking in the shadows waiting for some ghoul to attack.

A long form grew more opaque as it extended through the fog toward Amelia. Her heart skipped a beat and then she shrank back as the fog receded to reveal the head and body of a large elephant moving toward her. Amelia dug her gold lamé heels into the ground trying not to crumple, wondering how she was going to run.

"Your chariot has arrived." A deep male voice sounded in the fog.

Amelia looked around. Her voice unfulfilled by her breath held tight, Amelia could only silently worry. *Who said that?*

*I don't think you have to go very far to figure out that one. The waiter said something like that earlier this afternoon and now I am making the same offer of giving you a lift.* The voice was happening inside Amelia's head. Eyebrows sharply arched, she studied the elephant's left eye as it seemed to twinkle at her. *This is too weird,* she thought, as the elephant's enormous body broke through the fog. *You're thinking to me?*

*In a manner of speaking,* the elephant replied. *My name is Hrim, and I am not a bad escort for you to conjure up when traveling through this realm.*

The great elephant sidled up next to Amelia who backed away in short steps. A large howdah was perched on the elephant's back and strapped around his belly. A rope ladder extended toward her from the top. The elephant's skin was thick with creases and his legs and feet were as big around as Amelia's body. His toenails glimmered suddenly and mesmerized her attention.

*Nice, huh?* Hrim invited compliments. Amelia bent down to look more closely at the huge foot the elephant held up for her inspection. The nails were impeccably manicured and each was vibrating a different color of the rainbow.

"Very nice." Amelia nodded nervously though feeling a little less threatened by the beast. "You said I conjured you?" Amelia returned to the topic of the elephant's arrival.

*Indeed I did. Listen, why don't you climb onboard? I move very slowly through these parts and it would be nice to arrive at our destination before nightfall.* As Hrim finished his thought the fog began lifting.

Amelia felt herself engulfed with vertigo as waves of color and light moved into place producing the lush foliage and sounds of an Indonesian rain forest. The air became hot and humid. Touching her fingers to her brow she felt small beads of sweat quickly forming. Everything seemed so real.

Amelia regained her balance as she noticed her clothes had changed to a khaki safari outfit. She looked at her feet. The gold lamé shoes remained. *What the hell is that about?* Amelia started to stomp her foot and stumbled off her other heel. "Dammit!" She cussed as she kept herself from falling. The wild calls of birds were exchanged overhead in reaction to her shout. Amelia looked up and watched the treetops shift noisily as a pair of small monkeys chased each other across the limbs.

*Will you be joining me?* The elephant snorted even in thought.

"Where are we going?" Amelia turned to observe the trail she was standing on with the elephant. *Well I don't think it leads to New York City, but you never know.* Hrim eyed her carefully.

Amelia bent over slightly, patted her thighs and clapped her hands. "Zeke!" she called out, "Zeke?"

*I believe he's with Sherry and Jill getting a drink of water and having a little snack.* The elephant volunteered. Amelia reeled at the idea of the elephant knowing what was happening when she didn't know herself.

"This is a dream! My dream!" Amelia asserted. "How can you know what's going on in my private life?"

*I believe your little buddy already explained that one.* Amelia thought she saw Hrim smile.

11

"You're laughing at me?" Amelia cocked her head in Zeke-like fashion to take in the wide grin of the elephant. Shaking her head she desperately tried to stay on topic. "If you can know where Zeke is, why can't I?"

*But you do know now.* Hrim seemed to understand what was bothering Amelia. *This takes a little getting used to Amelia.* Hrim wagged his huge head and trunk around at the scenery. "Dreaming is an art," he said, then frowned, thinking, *though most humans consider it a novelty.*

Amelia squinted as she listened to the alternating blend of thought and spoken word. The elephant motioned his trunk toward the ladder. *I promise. You'll get better at this with time. You're right, this is your dream. What say we get on with it?*

Amelia looked at the elephant in utter disbelief. Tears welled up in her eyes.

*What?* Hrim lowered his head and eyed the tears as they drifted down Amelia's cheeks. *What did I say?*

"You didn't say anything." Amelia sobbed.

*Okay, so what did I think?* Hrim ventured again.

"I don't want to get better at this with time." Amelia broke into a full sob. "I want to know I'm going to be okay! I want to go home!" Amelia cupped her face in her hands and turned her back on the big beast. Amelia felt something soft brush against the back of her hands.

*Here. Take this.* She peeked through her fingers at a handkerchief held in Hrim's trunk. "Just a little something I dreamed up for you." Hrim tried a little humor as Amelia dabbed her eyes. *Listen. We're going to help you get home, don't you worry. But you're going to have to try and let me help. Come on now, climb on board and trust your imagination. It works even when your consciousness is on the blink.*

Amelia put her hands on the ladder. "I don't know what I'm doing," she said as she grabbed the ropes and started climbing to the top, "but I don't have much choice."

*Well, you're just starting out. Just keep an open mind.* The elephant's thought carried a reassuring feeling into Amelia's head and her heart relaxed a little. She climbed the ladder and arranged herself on the howdah thinking about how dreams never meant very much to her. *Usually I'm so tired by the time I go to bed at night that I'm too tired to dream.*

*You and everyone else in America,* Hrim replied. *But you're really just too busy to remember. Trust me, you dream.*

"Well at least I knew I was American." Amelia wondered how she could know these things but could not remember what sort of work or other endeavors kept her away from Zeke so much that she felt guilty and would dream him limitless treats. Then again she wondered if Zeke was her one and only memory or just a character in a dream. No dream she ever remembered seemed to be as vivid and inclusive as this dream.

*Let's play a little game.* Hrim suggested.

"Okay." Amelia tentatively agreed.

*Would you like a drink?*

"Yes, I would." Amelia noticed her throat was feeling dry.

*How 'bout a SNOWEE?* Hrim suggested. As Amelia thought about her favorite blue- colored treat from childhood, a cup filled with crushed blue ice appeared in her hand. "Whoa, that's a little like Bewitched!" Amelia scooped the already melting treat with a spoon.

*Better,* Hrim replied. *You don't have to do the nose-twitching thing.* Hrim paused for a moment, then added, *You must have always wanted to take a safari through the rainforest.*

"I love nature." Amelia wondered how she knew that.

*These things come back to you.* Hrim thought.

*What do I do for a living?* she asked. *Where do I live?*

*I'm sorry, but those questions seem to be out of bounds right now,* Hrim answered.

"What do you mean, out of bounds?" The howdah rocked as Hrim ambled down the jungle path.

*Well, it's your dream. You can bring to it whatever you wish at any time. Apparently you have brought a touch of amnesia to it if you can't remember who you are or what you're doing here.*

"But you knew I loved blue SNOWEEs."

*That's nice, but not exactly confidential information.* Amelia wondered what else the elephant might know about her habits. Remembering that Zeke told her she was in surgery, she tried for more information.

"Something happened to me. I don't remember that either. I need to find out what I'm doing here."

*That would be helpful.* The elephant nodded his head.

"But *you* can't be helpful?" Amelia couldn't conceive of how she could be expected to know what was going on in this dream by herself. Then again, she couldn't really expect an elephant to know either.

Hrim reached the end of his trunk back and patted Amelia on the hand reassuringly. She jerked her hand away yet felt amazed at the animal's compassion. *I'm sorry. I can't help with that yet. But you will make much better progress once you understand how things work. That must be our first order of business.* The pair grew silent for awhile as the howdah swayed back and forth. Amelia felt herself growing sleepy from the rocking movement and closed her eyes. She listened as the tall foliage pressing in from the edges of the trail was separated by the elephant's chest, parting and scraping along his legs and belly. It reminded her of the sound of a snail eating in its terrarium. Amelia's eyes popped open as she gave a little jump on the howdah.

*Careful there,* Hrim thought in calming tones. *Don't fall off.*

"I'm a teacher!" Amelia gasped. "I'm a teacher and I have a snail in my classroom!"

*Close, but no cigar.* Hrim shook his head. Amelia bristled at the elephant thinking it knew better than her.

"Of course I am!" Amelia insisted. "I remember a snail." She waited. "A snail named Dumbo!" she shouted. The jungle went silent. "And," she continued in elevated tones consistent with a great ah-ha moment, "I remember the sound it makes when it eats."

*Sorry.* The elephant wagged his trunk back and forth in the air. *You're picking up on someone else's dream.* Amelia tried to process what the elephant meant.

The rustling of the brush ahead on the trail caught Amelia's attention. She looked out but couldn't see what was coming.

"Hello? Hello!" a small boy's voice called out. Amelia looked down as the caramel skinned boy appeared below the elephant. He was dressed in a white cotton shirt and short pants. His head was wrapped in a turban and he held a feather and a clear rectangular container in his hand.

Amelia looked at the elephant expecting him to talk to the boy. The elephant stood silently gazing ahead.

"Can I help you?" Amelia asked. *As if I know what I'm doing here!*

"Is this Dumbo?" the boy asked. Amelia shot a look at the elephant and then back at the boy.

"Not exactly," she replied. "His name is Hrim."

"Can I have a ride?" he asked. The elephant continued to wait without participating in the conversation. Amelia looked at the boy and decided he seemed harmless enough. *A little more company couldn't hurt,* she thought.

*Wise choice,* Hrim thought to Amelia. Amelia looked down at the boy. He did not seem to have heard the elephant's thoughts.

"Okay, where to?" she asked the boy.

"The village," the boy replied, climbing up the ladder. He handed the feather and the small clear box to Amelia as he positioned himself on the howdah. Amelia looked inside the box. The bottom was littered with leaves and a snail shell hung from the underside of the lid, the snail evidently sleeping inside.

"That's Dumbo," he smiled. "I'm Jojo."

Amelia smiled back weakly, thinking. *And I am not a teacher. I*

15

*don't have a snail in my classroom. I don't know who I am or what I'm doing here. And I'm riding on an elephant in a little boy's dream.*

*We are going to the village,* Hrim thought to her. *You'll learn more there.* Once again Hrim began moving down the trail.

"Is that—is that it?" The boy's small face beamed at Amelia.

"Is that what?"

"This!" He cheered thrusting his arms in the air almost victoriously then peered seriously into her eyes as if he had just discovered a best kept secret. "This is the pace of a royal elephant!" he smiled.

*Pause, pause, pause...*

As the day progressed Amelia felt her body moving with the sway of Hrim's steps through the jungle. Her red curly hair glistened when the sun shot through the foliage overhead and lit up the howdah. She was noticing that things would change based on her thoughts. She sipped on her SNOWEE cup which seemed to endlessly renew its contents and watched Jojo playing with his snail.

Dumbo crawled from one hand to the other growing from his large marble size until he filled Jojo's hand like a baseball. Then the snail would shrink until it reached its original size again. Jojo held it in front of his eyes and watched it change colors. Like Hrim's painted toenails it shifted through the colors of the rainbow.

When the howdah was in the sunlight too long and Amelia began to feel hot, she wished for an umbrella and one appeared overhead to shelter her from the heat. For awhile she wished for music and she could hear all of her favorite songs playing one after another through a small boom box that materialized beside her on the howdah. Her dream seemed to be without condition except for allowing her to know why she was having it.

As they traveled, Hrim effortlessly moved through dense jungle, across a deep stream and now they were climbing high on a mountain path. The slope of the path was steep and the edge fell away sharply toward the valley below. Amelia tried not to look down. She wasn't afraid of heights as much as she was afraid of the edges between her and sheer drops. She couldn't stand to see someone standing on an edge. *All edges should have railings,* she thought. Just that quickly a railing manifested the entire length of the trail.

*That's really not necessary,* Hrim thought to her.

"I just thought a little safety net wouldn't hurt," she shrugged. Jojo looked at Amelia as if she had performed a great feat of magic.

"Ah, that is so cool!" Jojo looked at the railing and smiled at Amelia. "Do you really think that skinny piece of wood will stop this big old elephant from falling over the edge?"

Hrim's foot slipped on a rock. Amelia gasped for air.

Hrim caught himself from slipping into Jojo's imagining that he would fall. *Whoa! I really don't think ending up at the bottom of this precipice will further your interests.* Hrim thought to Amelia. *What say you get both your imaginations under control?* Amelia looked strangely at Jojo suddenly aware of having little experience with children.

"Let's just think safe thoughts," Amelia tried. "The railing made me feel safe but Hrim knows the way and he'll stay on the trail."

Amelia allowed herself to look over the edge. Below the railing the safety net she mentioned stretched across the entire valley and red fire engines were visible through the trees. It was as if she had imagined them to be on-hand in case of an emergency.

"I like fire trucks." Jojo smiled sheepishly. Amelia smiled back at the boy realizing the fire trucks were his idea. There was something that made her feel a little uneasy about being influenced by the imaginings of an eight-year-old boy. *There's no telling what he could dream up!* she thought.

*How about something like this?* Hrim stopped in his tracks and

Amelia looked forward. Walking toward them on the path was a huge Bengal tiger. Its eyes flashed neon green as it approached them holding its head low. The big cat stopped and sniffed at the air, then snarled and tossed its head from right to left. The tiger seemed not to be stalking as much as blocking the threesome.

"Jojo?" Amelia ventured, her eyes fixed on the beast. "Do you like tigers too?"

Jojo followed Amelia's gaze to the Bengal on the trail and jumped.

"Darius!" Jojo muttered in alarm. The Bengal cat was poised stealthily on the path. Neither the elephant nor the cat advanced. Amelia felt panic running through her arms to her numbing fingertips. Her skin was cold and the sweat from the heat became clammy. She eyed the tiger carefully.

"You *know* this tiger Jojo?" Amelia asked.

"Um-hmm." Jojo kept his eyes on the big cat as he breathlessly crept toward the front edge of the howdah.

"Is he friendly?" Amelia held out a hope.

"No ma'am. He's real mean!" Jojo whispered. Slowly, Jojo opened his hand and revealed the snail that again grew to the size of a baseball. He rolled the snail onto the howdah as it continued to grow. In a few moments Dumbo was as big as a coffee table and was crowding Amelia and Jojo on the howdah.

"Jojo," Amelia hissed, "I think I'm safer up here!" She gripped the weave of the platform. "Dumbo here is about to push me over the edge."

"Don't worry Miss Amelia. I'll save you!" Jojo sounded like a superhero in a Saturday morning cartoon, "I'll save you!"

*Was that an Underdog impersonation?* Amelia wondered.

Jojo stood up on the howdah and mounted his snail as if it were a horse. "Hi Ho Dumbo!" Jojo shouted pointing his arm into the air. The snail lifted off the back of the elephant and hovered over the howdah for a moment. Then the snail thrust his eye tubules periscopically upward and rocketed high above the trail. Dumbo skidded to a stop and snapped himself around to face the tiger like a missile waiting to be fired.

The cat crouched at the sight of the boy on the snail flying overhead. Slinking back several feet the big Bengal pressed its rear end into a group of rocks. The snail made a sound as if it were equipped with twin jet engines and swooped down toward the tiger. Amelia watched as the snail pulled up and almost grazed the tiger's head as it completed the pass. Jojo looked back over his shoulder and gave an excited shout. A moment later the boy and his trusty snail came about again and took another dive toward the tiger. His approach this time was from behind coming over the top of Hrim and thundering down the path toward the cat.

Amelia watched incredulously as the cat morphed ceasing to be a tiger. In its place crouched a large man with skin darker than Jojo's. He was dressed in a white t-shirt and too baggy pants that he held up with one hand as he started running along the path. He began yelling at the boy upon each pass.

"Back off, you! Leave me alone!" the man shouted and waved his free arm over his head.

Jojo paid no attention to his threatening tone. Clearly he felt in control of the situation. Again he blasted through the air toward his target, this time sporting a huge machete in his hand. Darius, the man, stood and prepared to duck when the boy came in swinging. He ran a step and turned to face the boy as he tried to calculate his best avenue for escape.

As the snail approached more closely, Darius looked over the edge of the path. He looked back at the boy who was toning a battle cry. Amelia sat on the howdah feeling her chest tighten as she watched the man climb over the railing and stand precariously balanced on the edge of the mountain. Jojo and his snail zoomed in for another pass.

Amelia barely shouted "NO!" as the man jumped up in the air and disappeared beyond the edge of the path. Amelia almost fainted as the snail proceeded over the edge after the man. Amelia heard

Darius yelling from below. She stretched herself flat on the howdah and peered over the edge toward the scene. Darius had landed in the safety net and was scrambling toward the edge on all fours. Jojo held his machete high in the air and flew the snail so it pounced at Darius again and again.

"Stop! Stop!" Darius shouted. "Stop it!"

"Oooo. Leave me aloooone!" Jojo mocked. "Get a-waaaay!" Jojo impersonated Darius and laughed as Darius fell to the edge of the net, and grabbing on, lowered himself to a treetop disappearing in the foliage.

Jojo and his snail hovered in the air for a moment apparently watching as Darius fled. Then Jojo turned and directed the snail to return to the high mountain path landing in front of Hrim. As Jojo disembarked his trusty steed, the snail shrank, returning to its normal size. Jojo picked up Dumbo and tucked him on top of his turban.

Jojo looked up at Amelia, his face bursting with a look of pride that spoke of a job well done. Standing in front of Hrim he asked for a ride. Hrim extended his trunk. The boy sat on the thick limb that curled around him, and Hrim began slowly walking along the path again.

Amelia glared at the boy half angry for the appearance of a tiger he apparently had manifested, half grateful that he had been able to vanquish the beast.

"Who's Darius?" she asked over the top of Hrim's head toward Jojo.

"Nobody," Jojo replied, "just a big ugly nobody." His small shoulders slumped just a little bit from his brave-chested posture just a moment before. For some reason Amelia didn't think they were through with Darius.

*Pause, pause, pause...*

*I need to spruce it up a bit,* Amelia heard Hrim thinking. The howdah shifted under her as it transformed from a simple piece of woven reed to become a much more lavishly appointed settee draped with a silken canopy. A basket appeared on the platform. Opening it Amelia saw it was filled with fruit. Looking over the edge of the howdah Amelia saw that Hrim's head was covered with an ornately woven tapestry of many bright colors.

*What's going on?* Amelia asked.

*We're almost there,* Hrim thought. *First impressions are very important.*

*What's this village like anyway?*

*We'll find out when we get there.* Hrim allowed for the imaginings of all involved and continued along the path.

Amelia let her head fall back against the edge of the howdah. In the distance she could hear music. She was unsure of what instruments were playing. *Perhaps a sitar and some sort of a flute?* she wondered as she rocked in the howdah watching a slight breeze move through the veils that made the canopy. Amelia listened as the sound of a village filled the air. At the edge of the village she listened as a mother chided her resistant child. As they grew closer in she could hear the calls of vendors reaching out for buyers. She could hear objects clinking together. They sounded like pots and pans in the kitchen of a restaurant.

Now from beyond the rim of the howdah she could see skinny, colorful, two-story buildings going by. Vendor's booths were shaded by large colorful stretches of fabric. Amelia sat up just as Jojo came over the top of Hrim's head and stepped inside the howdah. The marketplace was packed. People in long silken wraps and cotton materials examined the wares and foods available at countless booths that lined the road.

Though it didn't seem that anyone took particular notice of Hrim, he moved through the crowd effortlessly, albeit even more slowly as he approached an alley and turned away from the cacophony of marketplace sounds. Amelia looked around. The alley was empty and cool as the buildings on either side provided a clear path for the breeze and also complete shade from the sunlight. A man dressed in billowing black pants and a short vest that opened to reveal his smooth chest stepped out of a doorway. Amelia's eyes met with his. They were dark and deeply set under thick heavy eyebrows and wavy hair. She felt as if she knew him. He seemed to recognize her. There was nothing about him that suggested anything further. He didn't smile. He didn't turn into a tiger. She wasn't sure he was from her dream and not Jojo's, so she nudged the boy.

"Do you know this guy?" Amelia watched him for a moment. Jojo's eyes were fixed on the man as the boy seemed to study him with distrust. Either Jojo knew the man or just didn't trust men in general. Something in Amelia agreed with that idea and she wondered if she might actually know the man herself.

The man approached Hrim and moving to the side of the elephant and guided him to a sitting then lying position on the ground. Amelia and Jojo balanced themselves to and fro through the steep but smoothly executed movements. The man held up his hand beckoning Amelia to disembark the howdah. Jojo scrambled down on his own and looked up at Amelia. She reached out and took the man's hand. It was strong and supportive. She rested her forearm against his as she stepped to the ground in the gold lame shoes.

"The Guru has been waiting for you." The man spoke in a soft accent that seemed not to suit the setting. Amelia followed his lead toward the door then stopped. "What about Hrim?" she looked back at the elephant covered with a white layer of dust.

*I'll be fine,* Hrim reassured her. Amelia looked at the man. Like Jojo, he did not appear to have heard what the elephant thought. Amelia wondered if he could pick and choose who his thoughts became apparent to.

*It depends on where you're coming from.* Hrim attempted to answer. *They are not in the same place as you even though they are interacting with you.*

In her mind Amelia heard the voice of Judy Garland once again saying, *People come and go so strangely around here.* The man smiled and motioned invitingly toward the open door. Amelia looked through into a very dark room. She looked back at Hrim. *You'll be fine.* He nodded for her to continue. *Pay attention and learn.*

Amelia reached out and Jojo's hand slipped into hers as they disappeared through the doorway. The tall dark man followed after her.

*Pause, pause, pause...*

# 2

## *Guides, Gurus, and Guessing Games*

Hrim stood up and shook the dust from his deeply creased skin. *A bath would feel wonderful right about now,* he thought to himself. He checked up and down the alley to make sure no one was around as a shiver went through his body. Slowly his creased hide gave way and Hrim began to shift from a tall wide elephant to the form of a thin, short man clad in a white cotton robe with sandals on his feet. His bald head shined even though no sunlight was on it directly. His deeply tanned skin retained softer creases to match the age of fifty or sixty years. From beneath eyelids that had long stretched and fallen over his eyes, Hrim looked toward the doorway through which Amelia and Jojo had disappeared. "Be well." He softly voiced a simple blessing.

As he started back toward the marketplace another man clad in a similar white robe jogged toward Hrim. Touching him with a friendly gesture on the shoulder, the man slowed to walk beside him. "Hrim!" The man was happy to see him. "What are you up to these days?"

"Ah, Jahni!" Hrim embraced his friend. "Same old, same old." Jahni was younger than Hrim by at least twenty years. His soft sand colored hair was thick and neatly trimmed. His body was slender and muscular under the robe. He seemed to tower by six inches over Hrim as he grinned handsomely toward the old man.

"Still guiding?" Jahni asked.

"As ever," Hrim nodded. The pair stepped out of the alley into the crowded market. As they walked, the crowd parted before them, though none of the people seemed to take any notice of them. It was as if they moved without knowing why, or even knowing at all, that they were making way for the pair.

"Dreaming or dying?" Jahni asked. Hrim seemed distant. Jahni bent forward to look into Hrim's face. Hrim looked up and out at the sky.

"A little of both," Hrim acknowledged, then added, "Still too early to tell the final tally." Jahni nodded his head knowingly.

As they walked beyond the edge of the village the river became visible. Women were gathered on the shore, washing clothes for their families. Nearby a yak was drinking from the edge. A short distance beyond the usual riverside activities, several white cotton robes were hung on the branches of low lying trees and a party of men were bathing in the river. Hrim and Jahni walked upstream to join the group.

Hrim considered the thoughts he had read in the man's mind before leaving Amelia and Jojo in his care. *The guru will help her,* Hrim reassured himself. As Hrim prepared to hang his robe, some green Avadat finches lighted on the branches of the tree.

"Come," Hrim invited, and one of the tiny birds flew to his outstretched finger. "And they call you?" Hrim asked for the bird's name.

"Binga," the bird replied.

"Binga," Hrim repeated. "Would you be so kind as to pay a visit to Guru Tetta's house today and watch a friend who is on her journey there?"

"I am honored by your request, sir." Binga curtsied well for a bird, pressing her belly to his finger and then sprang into the air turning toward the village.

"Hrim," Jahni called from the water, "take a break! They'll still be there when you are refreshed!"

*Pause, pause, pause...*

The only light inside the house was from the narrow windows that looked out in the alley where Amelia and Jojo had left Hrim. As their eyes acclimated to the dim light, Jojo and Amelia were filled with wonder, each at different sights in the room. Jojo let go of Amelia's hand and sprang from her side as he raced toward a table filled with food.

"What's this?" Jojo pointed to a filled dish on the table.

"Jojo!" Amelia started to call him back to her side.

"It is okay," the tall, dark man reassured her. "He is hungry and the food is for our guests."

"Us? You were expecting us?" Amelia asked.

"Of course." the man replied.

"But how could you..." Amelia started to ask.

"How could we know?" the man completed her question. "Guru Tetta saw you in the distance and made preparations for your arrival."

Amelia looked around the room at men and women bustling throughout, arranging cushions and chairs, placing bowls of fruit and vases of flowers on low tables. Incense was burning which filled the room with a rich fragrance. A soft haze of dust from the streets outside floated through the windows on the light. A woman in a blue sari was pouring water from a pitcher into small bowls around the largest table. Amelia felt breathless as she took in the simple beauty of the room.

"Who is Guru Tetta?" Amelia asked, watching as Jojo sampled from the dishes. She closed her eyes and looked away as the boy pulled something back out of his mouth with a sour expression and dropped it under the table. *It's just a dream,* she thought.

"EXACTLY!" The voice of an older woman boomed behind Amelia, seemingly in response to her thoughts. Amelia turned on her gold lamé heels and managed to catch herself before she tripped. Looking down she avowed, *First chance I'm going to check the bazaar and get some more sensible shoes!*

"No." The old woman interjected and pointed to the shoes. "Those stay. They are important." Amelia looked at the woman and then at the shoes.

*These shoes are a pain in the,* Amelia checked herself, *feet!*

"They stay!" The woman dismissed Amelia's thoughts while slicing her hand through the air in a gesture that finalized the dialog. She brought her hand back toward Amelia offering to shake hands. "I am Tetta."

Amelia was speechless as she took in the commanding woman's features. Tetta was a round, but muscularly tight, light skinned woman with gray steaks running through massive dread locks of black hair pulled around her head and falling loosely down her back. A powerful force emanated from the woman's eyes, eliciting respect while conveying a deep sense of appreciation.

Amelia's escort cleared his throat and, thinking Amelia did not understand she was meeting her host, he bowed quickly toward Amelia and whispered, "This is the guru."

"And this is Miguel." Guru Tetta's expression revealed her amusement with his attempted subtlety as she gestured to the tall dark man. She turned and extended her hand again to Amelia. "Come."

Amelia missed the hand and looked at the dark man. *Miguel?* she thought. *That name doesn't sound like it belongs in this dream.*

"Well it does," Guru Tetta definitely replied to Amelia's thoughts, "and there's nothing I can do about *that*. It will connect for you in time."

Amelia looked into the woman's eyes. Finally connecting her hand with Tetta's, Amelia looked confused. "Aren't guru's supposed to be old men?" she asked. A titter of amusement circulated among the people in the room.

"I can see we have a lot to talk about." The woman raised Amelia's hand and led her toward the cushions beside the table.

The old woman fell onto her cushion with a deep sigh. A soft light fell on the side of her face from the window next to her. The other side of her face dissolved from a sea of wrinkles into shadows. Amelia startled when a chirping bird flew through the open window to land on the table in front of Tetta. The Guru looked intently at the bird as it chirped and hopped around in a circle on the table.

Tetta smiled and Amelia watched silently as the guru seemed to be listening to the bird's thoughts. Amelia watched as the woman's mannerisms seemed to morph between strong and decisive to deep gentleness and compassion. She felt safe in her presence.

"As you wish," Guru Tetta said to the bird, "and tell that old fart I said hello when you do." Amelia looked at the old woman curiously. Not only had she supposed all gurus were men but she also didn't imagine they would use the word *fart*.

"Eat," the woman invited, picking up a pierce of Chapattis. "You can dispense with the Guru and just call me Tetta." Her hostess was beating Amelia to what she was about to wonder by only milliseconds. "Guru is a title that simply means that you are here to learn." Tetta explained the salutation. "Some would still say a woman can't be a guru," Tetta mused. "But such politics are not why we're here." The old woman brushed the crumbs from her hands and placing them firmly on the smooth surface of the low table, she pushed herself up to stand. "You can't learn on an empty stomach or without rest, so eat. Elissa here will show you to a room when you are finished." The guru's gaze connected Amelia with a young woman across the room who smiled at Amelia. "Jojo will go with Miguel." She held up her hand to silence the speaking of Amelia's thoughts of concern for the boy. "Sleep and we will meet later." Tetta gently bowed a short movement toward Amelia and crossed into the shadows of the room leaving through a distant doorway.

Amelia looked around, then obligingly reached out for a piece of Chapattis bread. *What am I here to learn and how do I sleep during a dream?* she wondered.

*Pause, pause, pause...*

"So will you speak to my class?" Jahni asked Hrim as they dried themselves on the riverbank. The sun was warm and the breeze felt good on Hrim's back as he pulled his white robe over his shoulders.

"If you insist." Hrim didn't openly resist the invitation. Hrim preferred field work; it had been centuries since he had been a professor at University. After he took leave of educating the masses who showed up in the sleeping dream he took on individual apprentices who could consciously show up for class, and instructed them in their graduate field studies by giving them roles in teaching scenarios he selected from his caseload. In recent years Hrim had taken up working alone.

"Hrim, I don't need to tell you how valuable an hour of your stories could be to my students." Jahni piped in to the silence which was growing too long. He missed Hrim's presence in the halls of the most ancient school among all planes of consciousness. Like an aging male elephant, Hrim just didn't feel like running with the young boys anymore; he knew their tendency to defer to his experience kept them from developing their own skills.

"Well, perhaps we can make an exchange." Hrim offered. "I may need you to put on your dancing shoes little missy!" Jahni was reminded of countless rescues during which he played a dance hall girl in the wild west of the newly formed United States. "Not fair!" Jahni wrinkled his nose at the thought of all the high noon shootouts when he had played the loser's girlfriend in order to get him out of the dust and on his way to unfailingly pearly gates or hellfire of bonfire proportions. "I'd rather walk miles of endless highway hitching a ride as an undercover angel." Jahni dramatically referenced a legendary method Hrim had developed for keeping people out of the Wait Zone when it wasn't yet their time.

In the waking dream Hrim often appeared as that pivotal person that caught someone's attention and helped him or her have a synchronistic experience. In sleeping dreams he and Jahni had played as all forms of significant others in his project's lives. Hrim mused on the many tag team combinations he had played in with Jahni: mother, father, siblings, employer, partner, distant relatives, and neighbors.

Hrim had written the book on tapping into the memories of individuals stored in the space between the stars. He had chaired the committee on shape shifting, and produced the code of conduct for enacting the characters which would most benefit the human subject.

Hrim found metaphor to be one of the most effective tools serving both as major contributor to important life changes and as seemingly meaningless dream-stuff. Hrim appreciated the subtle energy of having appeared to Amelia as an elephant. It bypassed typical useless scenarios the human mind often associated with the Wait Zone by adapting a symbol that held interest for Amelia, it helped Amelia get to work as soon as possible. Thinking of useless Wait Zone scenarios reminded Hrim of how difficult it was to get new arrivals to let go of their pearly gate expectations.

"I could ask for a month of St. Peter duty." He laughed before Jahni voiced his objection.

"Oh no you don't!" Jahni nearly whined as a student given extra homework. "Let the newbies take on the book of life!" Project's expectations of having their lives reviewed by some authority in book format could take eons to clear through the Wait Zone if the subject was unwilling to awaken from their belief system and see the true configuration of life on the other side. Both Hrim and Jahni had more or less paid their dues which had landed Jahni the professorship and Hrim first pick of the most interesting cases.

Hrim had become aware of Amelia's presence as soon as she entered the fog. The circumstances of her arrival had been set-up decades before. Amelia was effectively comatose, neither dead nor alive. What would transpire in the Wait Zone would determine if she would awaken from the sleep that had engulfed her. As they strolled through the marketplace Jahni pressed Hrim for a commitment.

"This class is a group of new apprentices covering the illusion of good and evil."

"Some things never change," Hrim smiled and shook his head. The pair turned and entered an alley, stopped outside a worn and weathered wooden door and waited patiently. In a moment the door creaked open inward giving the two entry to a respite site for guides in the Wait Zone.

"If you are teaching," Hrim inquired, "what are you doing in the Wait Zone?"

"Field trip," Jahni replied. "I'll pick them up in a few hours."

"Okay then." Hrim slapped his hands together with anticipation of spending more time with his favorite student. "Let's get something to eat." The pair's joint imagining of some good home cooking morphed the respite area into a trucker's dream café. Their walk had been quiet and comfortable. Hrim was grateful. He knew most of Amelia's dreaming would not afford him much downtime. Not everyone in the Wait Zone was an etheric guide like Hrim. Many humans accessed the Wait Zone during average sleeping dreams when they were drawn there by the intensity of circumstances surrounding another person's presence there. Amelia had attracted many helpful, benevolent and not so helpful, malevolent entities to the Wait Zone. Hrim had called in Tetta to help him handle the overflow.

*Pause, pause, pause...*

*Dreams occur in the theta brain wave state. Lucid dreams are those during which the dreamer becomes aware he or she is dreaming and may take control of the dream. When one wishes to achieve a lucid dream experience they look for a predetermined sign or symbol that they are dreaming. When you see that sign, you will know you are dreaming and can set about creating the dream you desire. Some people love to take flight in lucid dream states. Others meet with long departed loved ones and sometimes help them reach the other side.*

Amelia didn't remember going to sleep. *Am I dreaming? My dreaming seems to be a documentary film.* Amelia strained to see in the dark auditorium. She adjusted her eyes away from the screen and momentarily was able to discern the shadowy shapes of heads around her in the audience. *Where am I?* she wondered. A section of shadowy heads three rows in front of her turned at once and *shush*ed at her in their thoughts.

*Okay!* she thought. *Sheesh, I'm new around here! I can't tell from one place to the next who can hear me thinking or not!* Amelia heard a few grumbles from distracted viewers around her. *Sorry.* She apologized, turned her attention to the screen and listened as the narration was thought-communicated.

*Astral projection is the ability to project one's energetic body away from the physical body. This is not necessary in the dream state as there is no physical body in dreams.* Amelia watched as a shadow figure on the screen seemed to eject a ball of energy from his

33

upper stomach area into the air. *Ewww!* She withdrew from the scene in her mind. Amelia pinched herself hard. There was no pain. *Am I astrally projected?* she wondered. The crowd in front of her *shushed* again. She thought of the pain she experienced when she first arrived in the fog. Something was different but she couldn't be sure what it was.

*When humans arrive in the WAIT ZONE they are assigned a guide. Guides often work within a family system for generations in order to facilitate personal evolution. Guides facilitate transitions and also work to keep anyone from crossing over before their time.*

Amelia perked up and paid close attention to the words that were rattling around her brain. Recognizing only a few of the terms the documentary was explaining, "Crossing over" was one that immediately struck a chord with her. *If I'm in the Wait Zone,* Amelia's thought voice quietly mimicked the intonation in the movie, *I don't recall meeting any guide.*

*Humans customarily enter into transition at a level of consciousness once called Purgatory or Limbo. Today this region of consciousness is generally referred to as the WAIT ZONE.* The words reverberated in Amelia's clenched jaws. *Because,* the voice continued, *humans hanging in the balance of life and death typically WAIT at this level until a guide can assist them.*

*Humans who have experienced this field of consciousness and returned to the waking dream often think they have experienced an intermediate stage to heaven or hell. Sometimes they report meeting a relative who told them it wasn't time yet and they needed to continue living. That relative was often a disguise for a guide intercepting the wayward traveler. Those who begin to move beyond to the next level of consciousness but then return to the waking dream often remember a bright white light and tunnel as their experience. When crossing out beyond the Wait Zone with an experienced guide the journey is completed to the next plane of consciousness awareness.*

34

*This film is produced by the University of Interplanar Consciousness.* Amelia's left eyebrow piqued at what sounded like a fake school offering bogus degrees on the internet. *Once, the only humans in the Wait Zone were there by necessity. All guides were etheric. Training for humans from the waking dream as apprentices in the sleeping dream to help in the WAIT ZONE was once inconceivable. But working with just a few has opened the doors for many to participate in a system of higher education that has been developed over the eons. What had once been gatherings of a very few souls is now a well-coordinated movement of thousands of souls to the University dream located at a beautiful between-level of consciousness.*

*With funding from the Universal Mind Center, the University offers students guided field trips to alternative dimensions of consciousness where they can resolve their karma and help others do the same. This inter-dimensional travel also serves as training for guide reserves who step up during periods of great activity on the WAIT ZONE brought about by disasters both natural and man-made, such as war. As you pursue your course of studies with the University there are certain issues we wish to address directly.*

Amelia scrutinized the screen images as scores of angelic guides floated to assist in hurricanes and battlefields. Her attention was drifting to wonder what her faith or religion might be when she detected the sound of snoring. She glanced around and identified the source as a man just about her age, sitting two rows behind her. *I guess he won't be graduating today.* She thought, and a few giggles broke out in the minds around her.

*Heh-m-m-m-m!* The movie continued as if it detected the distraction in the audience. Amelia looked up and watched the shifting shape of a human onscreen. *One of the most difficult things for human students to comprehend at University is the lack of form and gender among the teaching staff. Eternal guides -- those who NEVER lived a human life,* Amelia noted a tone of condescension, *are neither male nor female and not even young or old. They are, as they are needed to appear, according to the beliefs and challenges of their human projects.* Amelia wasn't keen on possibly being considered someone's project.

*They are the stuff of angels. Though they bear no wings, they can, according to one's belief that angels have wings, appear wearing them if necessary. What is essential is that a guide be able to engage the human spirit in the conscious use of its imagination. The goal of guidance is to get the human to break free of its limiting ideas and to open itself to receive Truth.* Amelia noticed she was slightly taking offense at the lack of gender allotted for humans in the narrator's vocabulary.

*Am I a feminist?* she wondered.

*Guides assume these roles in all fields of consciousness. However, in the sleeping dream-state and the WAIT ZONE,* Amelia covered her ears in an impractical attempt to dull the louder sound of the words, *everything, not just some things like synchronicities, but EVERYTHING could be symbolic of some need or issues from the person's waking life.*

Amelia wondered which, if not all, of her present circumstances might bear a clue that could help her find her way home…especially the golden slippers.

"Excuse me madam." An usher with an out-loud manner of speaking appeared in the aisle next to Amelia with a small flashlight pointed at the red carpet floor. "You have a call in the lobby."

"I do?" Amelia wondered who could be trying to reach her. She stood and stepped out into the aisle.

"Oui. Madam." The usher guided her to the back of the theatre with his little flashlight shining ahead of them.

The lobby was bright and filled with the aroma of fresh popcorn. Children were playing video games along the walls while clerks doled out candy and fountain drinks from behind the snack case. Amelia turned to ask the usher where she was but he was nowhere in sight. Four feet in front of her a phone was sitting on a clear acrylic pedestal. An amber colored hold button blinked on and off patiently as she gathered the call must be waiting for her.

Amelia advanced to the phone, picked up the receiver and pressed the blinking button.

"Hello?" she said.

"I have a long distance call for Miss Amelia Bradford," a voice announced. "Will you accept the charges?"

"Charges?"

"Yes. Shall I put the call through on your account?"

"Where is the call coming from?" Amelia asked

"Long distance ma'am. That's all I can tell you." Amelia looked up. The usher was standing in front of her.

"May I help you, mademoiselle?"

*Am I a Madam or a Mademoiselle?* Amelia wondered.

"I cannot say." The usher replied. "However, I can suggest you take the call."

"Yes, I'll accept the charges," Amelia agreed into the phone.

"Very well then," the operator replied. "You are being charged with negligence of your three-dimensional life and failure to show up and start your day." The operator paused. "Go ahead, sir." There was a brief clicking sound and then a deep male voice came on the line.

"Hello. Is this Amelia Bradford?" the voice asked.

"I suppose," Amelia replied, stretching her mind to see if Bradford might ring a bell as her real last name or if it was a name in dream only.

"Ms. Bradford," the voice went on, "we're trying to reach you. It's incredibly important that we hear from you soon." The call suddenly ended.

"Hello?" Amelia called into the receiver. "Hello?" She turned to see a finger depressing the receiver buttons on top of the phone. The finger was attached to a man who looked exactly like the manager of

37

the restaurant Amelia dreamed before she landed in the fog with Zeke. The manager was missing his cape and his horns, but he glared at Amelia in exactly the same way as he had when the waiter had pointed him out across the room.

"Excuse me Miss." The man addressed her with an ordinary American accent. "You're not authorized to use this phone."

"Excuse me?" Amelia questioned.

"That's quite alright," the man cut her off. "Now what are you doing here?"

"I'm not sure that's any of your business." Amelia tried to sound indignant. *I think I'll take my business elsewhere,* she tested to see if the man was privy to her thoughts. He seemed unaffected. She stepped toward the exit sign. He watched as she walked across the lobby. *Isn't he going to try to stop me?* she wondered. *Oh, I get it. He wants me to leave.*

Amelia's stubborn streak lit up, she turned on her heel and headed back toward the auditorium doors, but something was wrong. She stopped and looked down. The gold lamé shoes were missing.

*Pause, pause, pause...*

Amelia's body jumped as she awakened. Guru Tetta's warning tone sounded in Amelia's memory of their earlier conversation. "They stay," the guru had said of the gold lamé shoes. Amelia rolled over on a pile of pillows that molded to her body. She felt her feet click together. The gold lamé shoes were back on her feet.

Amelia thought of Judy Garland and Dorothy in the Wizard of Oz. She wondered if the shoes had some magical power to get her home. Amelia glanced around the room and remembered the place Elissa had taken her to after she finished her meal. It was small and everything in it was close to the floor. There was a long table on which sat a pitcher of water, drinking glass, bowl of fruit with chapattis bread and a vase of flowers. Cushions and pillows were arranged in piles near the table, but there was no one else in the room. It was clearly lodging for one.

Amelia removed the silken cover under which she had slept and sat up on the cushion stretching her legs out in front of her. Ever since she found herself in the restaurant she had been running on automatic. She had been suddenly whisked away, woke up in a fog, gone with Hrim down a path, picked-up Jojo, and met a guru in a remote village. The similarities to Dorothy's trip to Oz were piecing together. Fearing that they could be heading on a similar course, Amelia eyed the gold lamé shoes. The caped, horned-devil manager seemed as though he could be equated with a wicked witch and she didn't want to get into any altercations with him.

*Perhaps*, she thought, *I can cut to the chase.* She had to try it. Sliding, Amelia stuck her feet out over the edge of the cushion. Pressing the toes of the gold lamé shoes together she brought the heels together with a click three times and whispered softly, "There's no place like home. There's no place like home. There's no place like home." Amelia and the gold lamé shoes stayed very still on the cushion. They weren't a bad imitation of the ruby slippers, but they didn't do the trick. Her head slumped back onto her pillow.

*Who am I and what am I doing here?* Amelia thought. There was no answer. *Well, at least no one is listening in.* She tried to remember her dream but there was hardly a shred of it left in her memory.

*When you awaken*, she remembered a piece of the narration in the documentary, *try not to move or you'll change frequency and lose track of your dream.*

"Well, I guess I screwed that up." Amelia muttered. The image of the manager from the restaurant came to mind but she couldn't remember how he played into her most recent dreams. The glare in his eye remained penetratingly uncomfortable.

Of all the people she had thus far met on the road, she trusted the manager the least. Jojo certainly seemed harmless enough except for

39

his grandiose superhero dreams. Hrim made her feel safe. She hadn't quite come to a conclusion about Guru Tetta. Although his name was strange for the setting, Miguel seemed nice enough, especially to Jojo. Amelia stared up at the stars in the sky through her window.

Below the window a shadowy figure listened for any indication that Amelia was awake or what she might be thinking. The moment he saw her, he knew he was dealing with a delicate situation. He didn't think he would ever see her alive again. Now that he had been seen, he knew he needed to be very careful.

*Pause, pause, pause...*

Hrim shook his head and rolled over onto his left shoulder. The tapping continued near his right ear. Hrim flicked his hand across his face and a flutter brought him to bolt upright position on his cushion. He looked across the room and saw Jahni sleeping peacefully. Hrim held his arm in front of his face in the darkness. "Come." He whispered. Binga lighted on his hand and hopped up Hrim's arm to his shoulder and then leapt to the top of Hrim's head.

*What's this about?* Hrim frowned, eyes crossed looking up toward his forehead.

*The woman has a visitor!* The little bird nervously jumped back and forth from Hrim's head to his shoulder.

*Is she all right?* Hrim scrambled to his feet, slipping on his sandals.

*She hasn't seen him. He is hiding below her window.* Binga reported.

Hrim imagined a softly lit candle and held out his finger. Binga hopped on. *Be Still.* He instructed her with his thoughts. Hrim closed his eyes and focused on his breath for a moment then connected with the consciousness of the little bird. In the next moment Hrim's awareness was pressed through the walls of his room and projected beyond the restraints of time to the Guru's home on the other side of the village.

Beneath the window he observed the figure in the shadows. Moving past him Hrim flew up to the open window in Amelia's room and hovered there. Amelia lay on the cushion staring straight through him contemplating the coolness in of the night air. Hrim looked back to the ground. The man listened at the window a moment longer and then quietly headed down the deserted street breaking into a jog and disappearing around a corner.

Hrim turned back to see Amelia's eyes were drooping as she fell into her next dream. "Zeke?" she called softly. The shadow of a dachshund came through the wall and curled up on the cover at the end of the cushion. "Good boy." She cooed sleepily.

Hrim relaxed and perched on the windowsill glancing up and down the alley. There was a long way to go and he wasn't going to let anyone cut the story short if he could help it.

*Pause, pause, pause...*

The darkness was deeper than any Amelia had ever seen. Nothing was visible. She opened her eyes wider trying to see. With her arms stretched overhead she was clinging to something like a wall while fierce winds buffeted her back. She twisted her neck to squint out from under her arm. The wind stung at her eyes but she was able to see the stars as she had never seen them before. They were closer, and brighter.

*Other side.* A woman's voice spoke inside Amelia's mind.

"What?" Amelia shouted. She was having a hard time hearing over the roaring wind.

*I'm on the other side.* Amelia heard clearly inside her head. *According to the movie I just watched, so am I,* Amelia replied in thought.

*Very good. Lucidity already!* Amelia thrashed her body around as she tried to find a way to stop hanging on to whatever suspended her.

*Don't try to find a way, just wish to be here.* The voice replied. Amelia wished to join the voice and found herself sitting in front of Guru Tetta.

"Where are we?" Amelia asked, looking out at the black, star filled sky. The guru smiled. Amelia looked around. The terrain all around her was filled with craters. Amelia's jaw dropped. She tapped her teeth together and looked at the Guru. "We're on the moon?" she asked.

*Yes.* The Guru continued to think her words.

Amelia eyed the Guru. "Listen, I'm not used to talking to people who don't move their mouths. Could we *both* talk out loud?" she requested.

"As you wish," the Guru replied. "Where would you like to begin?"

"Why are we here?" Amelia motioned to the moon. She guessed she had much larger issues she would like to discuss with the Guru, but right now the question taking priority was why the audience had been granted on the edge of a mountain on the moon.

"It's not a mountain," Guru Tetta answered Amelia's thoughts. Amelia looked behind her and saw that the slope was just as deep and a little too close for comfort behind her as it was in front of her. Amelia's body gave a short, sudden wiggle as if to catch its balance.

"Crater," Amelia corrected herself. "Why are we meeting on the edge of a crater to talk?"

"This is not a crater," Tetta corrected again. "It is a precipice. The crater is waaaaay down there." Tetta pointed into the dark hole with her finger.

"I'm on an edge?" Amelia said aloud.

"Yes." The guru nodded and motioned as if Amelia should continue.

"This is a metaphor, a symbol?"

42

"Exactly!" The guru jutted her small fist into the air like a fan cheering at a baseball game.

"You brought me here to show me I'm on the edge?" Amelia felt her body position as if readying for a fight. "I could have told you that. I feel like I'm losing my mind!"

"No, dear," Tetta replied, "*Your* unconscious mind brought you here for several reasons." She laughed lightly.

"Such as?" Amelia simultaneously felt impatient and disrespectful but the guru didn't seem to mind.

"Partly because you thought you needed to climb a mountain in order to have an audience with a guru. Partly because, yes, the edge has meaning for you. And partly because of Jackie Gleason." Tetta looked intently into Amelia's eyes.

"Jackie Gleason?" Amelia repeated incredulously. "God, I wish that just one thing would make a little sense right now."

Tetta acknowledged the frustration mounting in Amelia. "You were thinking of him as you fell asleep remember? The man at your bedside, he looked like Jackie Gleason to you."

"Yes?" Amelia felt more and more confused.

"What was one of his best known expressions?" Tetta asked.

Amelia thought for a moment then her face relaxed. "To the moon, Alice?" she asked.

"As you wished." Tetta motioned to their surroundings.

"But I wasn't wishing for this," Amelia argued.

"That's just what we are here to discuss." Tetta sat down and arranged herself in easy pose in front of Amelia who suddenly realized there was nothing but air beneath the guru. "You humans have a lot to learn about the power of the word and you, my dear, must learn especially fast under the present conditions."

"So I'm on the edge," Amelia acknowledged. "The edge of what?"

"I cannot tell you this." Tetta shrugged her shoulders.

Amelia's red hair belied the flaring nature of her temper. As she felt the heat of anger and frustration rise she wondered if the guru would be aware of this as she was her thoughts.

"It's okay," Tetta acknowledged, "I could be angry if I were you. But I'm not and I am not keeping information from you child," the guru went on. "The things you are searching for are already in your grasp. You are simply not yet seeing them."

"More Wizard of Oz," Amelia mumbled, remembering her earlier attempt at clicking her heels together. "My ruby slippers are gold lamé, Guru," she commented.

The guru laughed aloud. "*That* was a nice try."

Amelia bristled. "You were watching me in my room?" Amelia shot an angry look at the Guru.

"No," the Guru answered. "Actually, I am not anywhere at least not in your usual sense. It is not necessary for you to think everything through. One word can convey a lifetime of experience."

Amelia felt herself grow regretful for the accusing outburst. "So what *can* you tell me if not what I'm doing here or how to get out alive?" Amelia asked.

"I can acquaint you with *where* you are." The guru advanced, "It could be very helpful for you to know how things work in this realm."

"Realm," Amelia repeated. "You say that as if this dream was a real place."

"It is." Guru Tetta stood on the edge of the crater and looked down at Amelia who felt uneasy inside just by watching the old woman walk on thin air. "Where we are and how it works may not seem the same as your typical dimension, but it is just as real."

"When I pinch myself it doesn't hurt," Amelia asserted as if feeling pain was some sort of a litmus test for reality.

"This is because you have moved beyond the boundaries of your physical body. You are actually beyond the bounds of space and time."

"So what's real about it then?" Amelia asked. The guru laughed and then caught herself as she picked up on Amelia's growing level of irritation.

"What you think you experience in your so-called three-dimensional world is no more *real* than all of this." Tetta explained. "It's just different. Everything you experience here or there comes about as the result of your own thoughts, words, and actions. You have limited yourself to 3-D measures of awareness such as pain. That doesn't mean that it isn't real if it doesn't hurt in this dimension."

"So we're in a *dream* world?" Amelia decided.

"You are in another area of consciousness. In your three-dimensional body you think all of this is happening outside you. Here there is no such standardized duality as inside and outside. Everything you conceive becomes your experience as you wrap your consciousness through it. When you experience your oneness with it you may experience your oneness as separate, but that is a choice. Can you see that?" The guru paused.

Amelia considered her words. They seemed to tear down as fast as they built up an example. In her heart Amelia became aware that she rarely remembered her dreams in 3-D life and didn't have much interest in other realms or planes of existence.

"Well it's time to give it a try." Tetta addressed Amelia's thoughts.

"Do you mean that my experience of you happens inside me?" Amelia responded.

"Take out the *you* and *me* and you get it."

"Experience...happens?" she asked.

"According to your beliefs which are thoughts that act like silent words to create your experience. See?" The guru Tetta smiled.

"Then I should be able to change my thoughts and change my experience, correct?" Amelia eyed the Guru.

"Yes."

"Then what am I still doing here? I have wished myself out of

45

this place, home with my dog and yet I remain. What's the deal, Guru?" Amelia felt strangely confrontational and extremely uncomfortable about it but held her position forgetting Tetta was privy to her every thought and feeling.

"There is a system of checks and balances my dear." Tetta explained, "Apparently there are many more thoughts and wishes that have brought you to this point which outweigh your recently manufactured desire to retreat."

"Retreat? You make it sound like I'm giving up." Amelia noticed how her ego bristled at the idea of quitting. *I must be a fighter,* she thought.

*You are.* The guru thought back in the calmest most reassuring thought form she could send out. *That is why you are still here.* Amelia silently gazed into the guru's eyes as she realized just how slight the difference between going home and fully crossing over must be.

"I'm just trying to figure out how I can fight if I don't know what's going on. How can I know what's safe?"

"There you go with duality again!" The guru pointed at Amelia. "You wouldn't be here if you needed to be safe. This is a whole-hearted, winner take all event you have entered into. The key is to give up the need to be safe."

"Why should I?"

"Because the amount of energy you need to expend on the illusion of being safe is also what you need for a break-through." Tetta let the side of her fist land in the palm of her outstretched hand for effect. "All attempts to protect yourself eventually produce only the illusion that you are safe." Tetta underlined her words with the tips of her fingers as she spoke. "That's what got you here and it is now time to stop for your own sake and the sake of everyone involved!"

"We're never safe?" Amelia ventured.

"Never." Tetta replied. "But we're never truly in danger either," she reassured.

"But people are physically hurt all the time."

"Yes, but that is not your limit."

"Well, I guess that depends on my beliefs."

"Correct. If you believe you are limited to your body for existence then you will attempt to stay safe, which is to avoid and cut yourself off from the Truth."

"And the *truth* is?"

"That everything is one, everything is connected. If everything lived from that truth then everyone would be able to hear everything all the time."

"That could get very confusing." Amelia shook her head.

"It can seem overwhelming," Tetta nodded, "which feels unsafe to many, so they shut themselves off."

"So I still don't get how I can benefit from not being safe."

"Because then you'll be able to have awareness of your reasons for being here." The guru moved her face closer to Amelia's and pressed her eyes to meet with hers. "If you maintain the need to be safe then you must remain ignorant of the agreements and arrangements you made for this journey; and the likelihood of accomplishing your goals will remain diminished, even improbable."

"So what do I do instead?"

"Give up the need to be safe, stop relying upon your limited thoughts and beliefs, and let yourself be in the flow."

"How?" Amelia could not consider the possibility of not thinking. Her thoughts were constantly active. A benefit, she believed.

"Think about the boy and the tiger." Guru Tetta looked deep into Amelia's eyes. In the pupils of the guru's eyes, the entire scene of Darius as the tiger showing up on the mountain path replayed as if it were a movie. "Very good," the guru concluded, "then you see."

"See what?" Amelia asked urgently, afraid the Guru might be ending their conversation.

"See that no harm came to anyone on the mountain," the guru

proclaimed. "See that the elephant did not need a railing." Tetta held up one finger as if keeping count. "The boy entered into the flow. He was not afraid." The second finger sprang into place. "He took care of the tiger with ease." Another finger went up. "On his suddenly large and flying snail." She continued to raise fingers in a counting motion. "Even when the man fell over the side *he* landed safely on a net." Tetta held up four fingers. "Four things that could have gone wrong because the boy was in the flow." She dropped her hands to her hips and gave a little jump for emphasis.

"So no one can really be harmed in a dream?" Amelia asked.

The guru slapped her hand to her forehead in frustration. "Real is a dream," the guru replied. "Every time you dream in your sleep you leave your body. You are dead to your body. Free of it." Tetta searched for the right words to connect with Amelia on the subject. "Dying is dangerous in 3-D only because humans perceive the loss of their bodies as the end of their existence. But that is not the end of you, sure as you are here talking with me now."

Amelia was more confused than when they began. She remembered that in the fog before her experiences in the jungle Zeke had told her she was having surgery. "Can my physical body die while I'm here?" she asked.

"Yes," the guru replied, "There are two ways. You leave your body for good or you believe you can't get back."

"Why would I believe that?" Amelia asked.

"Have you been able to return so far?" the guru pointed out.

"But I want to get back."

"Wanting leaves you wanting. When you have cleared what you have put in place to keep you safe then your wanting will be over and you will be wherever you are," the guru admonished.

"Then I could just wake up?" Amelia asked.

"When you have your yellow bricks in a row," the guru borrowed the metaphor. "You have reasons for being here now which only you can tell. To understand these reasons will be easier when you know more about how this realm works. Can we get on with it?"

Amelia was exhausted. She felt challenged and a little beaten up. She couldn't conceive how the information the guru had so far given her might help her remember who she was or what she was doing here, but she felt limited to the present circumstances. Slowly she realized it was her acceptance of this limit that could leave her hanging short of a solution yet again.

"Teach me more." Amelia looked at the guru with refreshed determination.

*Pause, pause, pause...*

3

## *Don't Let the Parade Pass You By*

"Wake up!" Amelia felt her shoulder being pulled back and forth, rocking her whole body. "Wake up!" Jojo kept pulling.

"No, Jojo, NO!" Amelia pulled her head down toward her chest trying to hold on to her sleep. *That's silly,* she thought, *what sleep?* Her dream began to fade.

"The parade is coming!" Jojo exclaimed, "And there's a whole bunch of Dumbos!"

Amelia felt her silky nightgown turn into flannel pajamas out of modesty in front of Jojo. She rolled over onto her back. "When, where?" Amelia asked.

"Right now!" Jojo jumped to his feet and scrambled to the window next to Hrim whom he didn't see.

Amelia looked at the ceiling and tried to remember her dream. With a sense of futility it slipped past her recollection and all she was left with was the image of the guru standing off the edge of a large crater in mid air. She heard Tetta's last words: "Zen says: *Leap and the net will appear,* but this is more true: *Leap and the need for the net will disappear.*"

"Come on, come on! Before it's all over!" Jojo's feet danced on the floor as he frantically tried to get Amelia to join him before the parade passed by. Amelia smiled at Jojo, her eyes also overlooking the sketchy presence of Hrim's consciousness as it receded to his cot in the respite area.

"Come and look!" Amelia's eyes moved up to Jojo's face and she saw that something was different. She looked around the room. Everything was different.

Amelia pushed herself into a sitting position. She was in the middle of a double size bed with a down comforter. The room was decorated with curtains that reminded Amelia of a country cottage. She sprang from the bed still clad in the flannel pajamas and looked past Jojo out the window.

A wooden framed porch stretched beyond sight outside the window. Beyond that a small green lawn was neatly trimmed and edged with red geraniums. Small groups of people cheered along the edges of a normal looking Midwest America street as a parade did indeed pass by.

Amelia listened to the playing of a small brass band. The music was celebrational and the instrumentalists strutted with their knees high in the air. They wore red uniforms with long tails in back and big brass buttons hitched with yellow straps in front.

Following the musicians a wagon was being towed by a huge elephant and followed by many more elephants. Amelia looked at the side of the wagon and blinked her eyes for clarity. In yellow letters on the red paint were the words Drury Brothers Circus Extravaganza.

Amelia pulled her head back inside the window. Once more, even more than the night before, she didn't know where she was or what she was doing there. *Is it possible?* she wondered. Amelia looked for the gold lamé shoes. They were still on her feet. *Guess*

*I'm still in the shoe realm. I must be getting used to these,* she thought as she considered the ease with which she sprinted to the window.

Amelia stepped back. "Isn't it cool?" Jojo looked up at her. "A circus! I've never been to a circus before!"

Amelia looked into the boy's beaming face and relaxed enough to smell the coffee and bacon that was being cooked somewhere inside the house. She looked down and instantly found herself clothed in a white blouse and blue slacks. Jojo didn't seem to notice her fancy dressing skills. Amelia heard a dog bark and turned once more to look out the window. Zeke stood wagging his tail in the yard. "Guess what Dorothy?" Zeke teased. "It looks like we made it to Kansas.

"Very funny!" Amelia rolled her eyes at the dog.

"What's funny?" Jojo asked as Amelia realized he couldn't hear or understand Zeke.

"Good morning." A voice came from the doorway. Jojo and Amelia turned. Standing inside the white doorframe of the small country cottage, Miguel looked larger than the night before. His vest and billowing slacks were exchanged for a more casual pair of jeans and light denim shirt. "Did you sleep well?" he asked.

"Yes." Amelia wondered if Miguel or Jojo noticed the differences she was experiencing. It didn't seem like it since no one was acknowledging it in any way.

"Tetta would like you to come and join her," Miguel invited.

*At least the guru is still around.* Amelia thought as she followed Miguel down the hallway. Jojo caught up and shot past the pair.

"He's been up for awhile," said Miguel explaining how Jojo knew where to move in the small cottage.

The couch in the living room was covered in heavily decorated tapestry material. A crocheted doily covered the back. A curio cabinet on the wall displayed countless Precious Moment statues and a wooden rocking chair sat near a stone fireplace next to the front window.

Amelia surveyed the decor as they crossed into the dining room that, in addition to the maple table and chairs, had a piano and a china cabinet. Through the swinging door into the big eat-in kitchen Amelia saw Jojo talking to an elderly woman who was arranging bacon on a plate next to the stove. Her apron was white over a yellow blouse and green slacks.

"Would you like some coffee?" Tetta turned and smiled at Amelia. The guru had turned into a granny. Her long dreadlocks had been replaced with a long braid. Her hair seemed to have become more gray. The accent that had seemed appropriate in the village had been replaced by one with a distinct southern texture.

Tetta pulled a white painted bentwood chair out from the kitchen table just in time to catch Amelia's sagging figure. Fresh flowers and a bowl of fruit were arranged on the table along with perfectly set place settings of white china and glasses filled with orange juice.

*Everything's different and yet everything's the same,* Amelia thought.

*That's the way of everything isn't it?* Tetta was still privy to her thoughts which became something of a comfort to Amelia.

*How can that be?* she thought-spoke with Tetta.

*Oh, even where you come from, change is the nature of things. You only think ev'rything is the same. It never is. Your mind holds a memory of ev'rything being a certain way and so it seems to be true, but ev'rything, ev'rything is constantly changing.*

*Well,* Amelia thought, *it doesn't usually seem to change this drastically. One minute we were in India, now we're in Main Street, America.*

Tetta shrugged showing a curious smile and raised eyebrows. *That's the dream you seem to be havin'."*

Amelia looked around at the country kitchen, then down at the gold lamé shoes. *My dream is somewhere between these two extremes? And how is it that Jojo's dream has shifted with mine?* Amelia thought about Hrim. *He must be following the elephants.*

She wondered if Hrim could now be one of the circus elephants. Amelia looked to Tetta for some indication which was not forthcoming as the guru-turned-granny placed a cup of coffee on the table followed by a sugar bowl, spoon and fresh cream.

Amelia felt something lightly touching her finger. She looked just as the pretty green and yellow bird hopped onto her hand. She raised her hand in front of her face. *Who are you?* she wondered. *I am Binga!* the little bird replied in thought.

"Binga," Amelia repeated, feeling herself continue to struggle with the thought talking and thinking with animals.

Jojo admired the little bird on Amelia's finger. "Hey little bird," he whispered, "maybe you can come with us when we go to the circus."

*Pause, pause, pause...*

*To summarize, the forces of good and evil are nothing more than a construct of the human mind, developed as it learned to manipulate the Earth plane. In the grand scheme of things it is counter-productive, but there is little that can be done about it as the group consciousness maintains this illusion.* Hundreds of Jahni's white robed students were learning the ropes of being guides as Hrim gave his presentation. Hrim felt he had conveyed his message as the protestations of thought had quieted during the talk.

*We must all find a way to deal with the ever shifting illusion of what is good to some humans and evil to others. Humanity is just beginning to break the bonds of being vilified and victimized by the judgments that fall into the limiting, lack-luster, categories of Good and Evil.* Hrim's thought speech emphasized key expressions and planted them in the minds of Jahni's dreaming students so they would re-experience the concepts later in their waking life.

*The dualistic world is dependent upon two seemingly opposing forces through which the tug-of-war suspends the illusion of form.*

*Humans have confused this need with the actual causes of war, good and evil, each claiming an interest in ending suffering, both actually work to continue it. One does so by focusing on suffering as wrong and strives to change it; the other sees suffering as an inevitable outcome of wrong which must be changed. Tit for tat.* Hrim alternately tapped the back of each hand.

*What needs to change is the belief in, need for, and fear of suffering. Then judgment and its good and evil tools will become obsolete. It is up to us to find small, progressive ways to help humans comprehend this is a colossal waste of creative expression. All of creation is perfect. Even when the appearance of something is imperfect, it nonetheless perfectly appears to be imperfect.*

*Beneath its seemingly unchanging conditions, the Earth plane and all the consciousness that makes it up is shifting. Changes long awaited are currently precipitating and soon we will be joined by countless newcomers who will require assistance. Of course, the cause will be neither good nor evil, but many will use it as the evidence to support their side of the story; and that is what we will have to work with here.*

The auditorium murmured at the thought of soon needing to implement their studies. Jahni started walking down the aisle as Hrim concluded his presentation.

*It has been a pleasure to join you for this impromptu talk today. It is good to see so many souls gathering to take on the work we are now facing. Meanwhile, I have a case that is very much about the nature of the human being as I have described today. And it is time I rejoin my subject. Which reminds me to remind you, when working with your people it is important to stay close and know that once they cross over, whether temporarily or permanently, they really have no training as to how it works. They've been going about their whole lives wondering what they were doing on Earth. Then they come into the dimensions we know so well still not knowing what they're doing. So, be present, be firm, and be gentle.*

Hrim gave a short bow to the audience and a cacophony of applause rose from the room. Jahni greeted him as he left the podium.

"My friend, you are an inspiration to me and my students." Jahni hugged Hrim.

"Truly, my pleasure, Jahni." Hrim put his hand on Jahni's shoulder.

"You are on your way then?" Jahni looked eager to learn the state of Hrim's case.

"Yes," Hrim rolled his eyes and sighed as he scanned the field. "Off to the circus and not just a few unexpected interruptions."

"You should be used to that by now," Jahni called after Hrim as he left the stage of the auditorium and disappeared into the dark folds of the curtains.

*Pause, pause, pause...*

After breakfast Tetta and Amelia walked along Main Street as Miguel hung back with Jojo who was investigating every curious thing he saw in the front yards they were passing.

"This place seems so ideal," Amelia commented, not really understanding what she was picking up on. "Everyone seems to be having the perfect American experience," she noted, "like the 1950's come back to life."

"A good assessment," Tetta replied. In almost every yard children were playing, often accompanied by a parent. Moms were wearing brightly colored dresses and dads were actively teaching youngsters to ride bikes or fly kites. Several young couples were walking along Main Street hand in hand. Amelia and Tetta passed a small group of polite teenagers tending to ice cream cones and slurping chocolate malts outside the corner drug store. "Everything is as perfect as it can be," Tetta agreed.

From the end of Main Street Amelia could see the circus people setting up the big top. Jojo shot up next to Amelia and walked beside her. "Can we go see the animals?" Jojo looked up with pleading eyes. Amelia couldn't figure out when she became like a mother to Jojo. She really didn't feel the protective instinct she thought she should feel if she was his mother. "Please!" the boy pleaded.

"Why don't you go with Miguel?" Tetta suggested. Jojo turned and shot back down the street meeting Miguel. Grabbing Miguel's hand Jojo started swinging and pulling his lengthy arm moving Miguel toward the circus scene.

"C'mon Miguel! Let's go see!" Miguel trotted awkwardly behind the boy being careful not to step on him.

"Okay, Okay!" Miguel turned and waved at Tetta and Amelia. "We'll see you later." The pair watched the man and boy jog toward the circus wagons in the distance.

Amelia looked down into her hands and found she was holding Dumbo the snail. *He must have been afraid he would lose it*, she thought.

"Actually," Tetta read her mind, "I think he wants you to be safe."

*Why would Jojo think I needed to be safe?* Amelia thought then looked to see if Tetta might reply. Tetta smiled back at Amelia but no further information was offered. Amelia looked deeply into Tetta's eyes then up at the sky, which seemed bluer than usual and was completely free of clouds. "Did *I* dream this?" she asked Tetta.

"No, you didn't dream this," Tetta replied.

"Then who did?" Amelia asked. "You?"

"Heavens, no."

"Then who?"

"If you must know, it is your mother." Amelia was surprised at the information that was shared.

"I have a mother?"

"Most humans do." Tetta laughed.

"Well I know that, but I can't remember my mother right now. Is she here?" Amelia imagined that her mother could be in her dream the same way as Jojo showed up.

"No dear, she can't be here."

"Why not?"

The two strolled past the barber shop on Main Street. Tetta paused as if she was listening to something. "She doesn't believe she can reach you right now."

"What did you just do?" Amelia asked.

"Humm?" Tetta avoided the answer.

"Just then," Amelia insisted. "You seemed to be listening or checking in with something. What is it?"

Tetta sighed in acknowledgement of what Amelia had noticed. "I was checking along the web." Tetta answered.

"The what?" Amelia wondered how Tetta could check the internet without benefit of a computer. "How did something about me get posted on the web?" she asked with a tone underlining a sense of privacy violation.

"The zone, the field, the ethers ...," Tetta clarified, "of consciousness?" She stopped trying as Amelia shook her head and frowned at the foreign concept. "It's a miracle you made it here alive," Tetta mumbled. Sighing, she took a seat on a bench and patted the space beside her.

"Sit here," she instructed. Amelia took her place. "All that has ever happened is energy recorded in space." Amelia nodded to indicate she understood basic scientific law. "The energy and the space are the same thing just possessing different textures." Amelia nodded a little more hesitantly.

"All of this space energy together is consciousness, the One Consciousness." Tetta eyed Amelia to see if she was still following along. Amelia's eyes appeared a little glazed over but Tetta continued. "This conscious energy moves in and between all that IS, in moments so small the shifting can't be detected."

Tetta stopped and looked across the street. Amelia snapped out of her lull and followed Tetta's gaze. She thought she saw the shadow of a man stepping around the corner. She waited a moment as if he might return.

"Was that Miguel?" Amelia asked. Tetta seemed to be checking in with the ethers again.

Amelia tried to get Tetta's attention. "I don't understand how this relates to what my mom is dreaming for me or why she doesn't believe she can reach me." Amelia glanced back at the alley, no one was there.

"From you here in the now to your three-dimensional body and beyond, there is a thread of energy which I may locate and follow. That thread is woven with all of the threads you are connected to. I simply followed the thread to your mother and ascertained that she is currently dreaming about you."

"But why did she dream me here?"

"Amelia, your mother always wants you to be safe so she has dreams of you in safe places. Can you think of any place safer than this hometown atmosphere? For your mother, this is a symbol for safety."

"Jojo's worried about my safety. My mom is dreaming me in a safe place. Why am I not safe? Is there a problem with my body?" Amelia asked.

"That remains to be seen," Tetta replied. Amelia felt a spark of rage flash under the surface.

"But you just said you could follow the thread back and find out." Amelia wanted to know more.

Tetta nodded. "I can, but the information is out of bounds right now, yet to be decided by the choices you will soon make."

"That sounds ominous!" Amelia heaved a huge sigh. Holding out her leg she looked down at the gold lamé shoes still stuck to her feet. "I wish these shoes would go out of bounds!"

"In time they may and then you will know everything." Tetta stood and took Amelia's hand. "Everyone is rooting for you Amelia, so remember you have no need to waste any of your own precious energy on trying to stay safe," she said. "Walk home with me. There is a community picnic today and I need to prepare our basket."

Amelia stood and walked with Tetta. She felt like a guest in her own dream... or rather her mother's dream for her. She was amazed at the way everyone else seemed to adapt so easily to the new environment and activities that needed to be carried out. She looked at all of the families socializing. She wondered if they were all dreaming too.

"Indeed they are dreamin'." Tetta acknowledged Amelia's thoughts. "These, and all those who adapt easily, are dreamers who won't remember much of their dreams tomorrow morning. They will say things like, 'I was in a town I didn't recognize and there was a circus that came through.' For many of them the circus will turn out to have significance in relation to some area of their life. The circus might represent the way things seem at work for instance. This may or may not be an accurate association, but for those who remember it may seem to be helpful."

"I don't usually don't remember my dreams." Amelia felt as if she was almost confessing a sin to Tetta. "Am I usually playing one of these supportive roles then?"

"Perhaps," Tetta acknowledged. "Then again, maybe you just haven't needed to remember."

*I need to remember now.* Amelia thought. Tetta hummed in agreement.

"Sometimes we try too hard. The important thing is to flow and be in our present experience. Then we will be paying attention when important things unfold."

"Are you saying that I might find the secret to what's going on with me in the dream rather than by trying to wake up?"

"Yes, I am saying that." Tetta nodded. "Only you can bring what is out of bounds into focus and until then your *safe* place is in the dream."

The words confused Amelia, but she knew it was a sort of riddle that Tetta would not further explain. She thought of the mother she could not remember and decided that fully conscious of the process or not, she would send a message to the woman who had dreamed this safe place. *I'm okay,* she sent out into the ethers. *Mom, I'll be home soon.*

*Pause, pause, pause...*

The picnic grounds were far on the other side of town. Tetta had prepared a huge basket containing fried chicken, potato salad, and cornbread. Amelia carried a pitcher of iced tea that had brewed in the sunlight on the front porch. The pounding sound of feet stomping on the ground signaled that Jojo was approaching from behind undoubtedly ready to share exciting news of all he had witnessed as the circus was setting up.

Jojo slowed to a walk beside Amelia. He turned his head and looked up at her panting with his tongue sticking flat out to dramatize how fast he had run. A big smile broke across his face.

"Where's Miguel?" she asked.

"He needed to go someplace else." Jojo heaved with over-exaggerated breaths. "He said he'd see us at the picnic."

"Oh, I see." Amelia noticed that she felt disappointed. *Don't get caught up in Miguel, sister,* she thought to herself. *He's only a dream.*

As Jojo rambled on about the circus, Amelia's thoughts again turned to the possibility that Hrim was one of the elephants at the circus. Since she knew Jojo couldn't talk with Hrim she didn't ask. She wondered if she would be able to recognize him among the other elephants.

A small service station was the last business on the edge of town. Two very old-fashioned looking gas pumps that still sported rolling numbers on the display stood on a cement island. An old man in gray coveralls had just completed a full-service fuel transaction as the threesome approached.     He deftly wiped the wind-shield wiper blade and laid it on the glass.  Patting the top of the car as it rolled away the man looked up and smiled at Amelia.

"Morning." The old man removed his hat to reveal his bald head and took a swipe at his brow with a red bandana.

"Afternoon," Tetta corrected him.

"Afternoon?" the man replied in a teasing tone.  "Already?"

"Are you coming to the picnic today Hiram?" she asked.

"I s'pose that would be a very nice way to spend my day." Hiram stepped forward. "What ya' got packed in that pretty basket, Miss Tetta?" The man's accent seemed to be getting thicker and even, Amelia noted, a little overdone.  She wondered what brought him to the dream with knowledge of Tetta's name as he poked his finger under the linen that covered the basket.  Leaning close, trying to see what's inside, Hiram looked up at Amelia and winked, then extended his hand and stepped closer.

"I'm just fooling around," he said. "My name's Hiram."

"Pleased to meet you." Amelia shook his hand and felt more connected to the man than as if this was their first meeting. *Maybe he was in my dream last night,* she thought.  There was no thought-reply from Tetta or anyone else.  She felt she must have struck on something and decided to pay close attention to the man.

Hiram shot a mischievous glance sideways at Tetta and let go of Amelia's hand.  "Just let me close up the store and I'll walk the rest of the way with you." He trotted across the pavement toward the office of the service station. Amelia looked to catch Tetta's eye, but the old woman didn't look.  Tetta's earlier words came back with deeper meaning now, *Only you can bring what is out of bounds into focus and until then your safe place is still in the dream.* Sometimes Amelia couldn't tell if she was remembering or hearing think-speak.

Hiram rejoined the group and the foursome walked slowly amid several other clusters of picnic-goers.  Amelia marveled at how well Jojo got along with everyone.  He seemed to know exactly what to say to whomever he met and was quite adept at turning on the charm to get what he wanted. Hiram seemed equally good at acclimating to his new young friend.

"How 'bout a round of horse shoes when we get to the park?" Hiram asked Jojo.

"Horses wear shoes?"

"Indeed they do little fella'. Big metal shoes shaped like the letter U."

"How do they get their feet in them?" Jojo danced backward in front of Hiram as he asked him questions.

"They stand on them."

"Ohhh." Jojo pretended to understand, then asked, "and then we make them around their feet?" Hiram laughed heartily at the boy.

*So he's not exactly from the country,* Amelia observed of Jojo's knowledge of animals and horse shoes.

At the picnic grounds, the clusters of people gathered under a classic beautiful hometown-America-style grove of apple trees with plenty of shade for everyone. A nearby group of picnic tables was central command for all of the dishes that people brought to share. As Tetta spread a blanket under the shade of a big apple tree, Hiram and Jojo advanced to the horseshoe courts while Amelia added their food to the main table.

"I don't know how to play horseshoes," Jojo worried.

"There's nothing to it," Hiram reassured him.

"Don't the horses get mad?"

"The horses aren't wearing these shoes anymore," Hiram explained.

"So where do we throw them?"

The pair's voices were growing softer as they got farther away from the table.

"You try to get them to go around a little iron spike in the ground."

"Why?"

"It's like a touchdown," Hiram compared.

"Ooohhh." Jojo seemed to understand for the moment.

Amelia's eyes rolled skyward. "Jojo has a million questions in him." She turned toward Tetta. "We've been gone a long time. Shouldn't Jojo's mom be worried about him?"

"We're beyond time," Tetta replied, removing the plastic lid from the container holding the potato salad. She shooed a fly and Binga flew from a nearby branch to chase after it.

"Tetta, why do you think Jojo stays with me even though my dream has changed?" Amelia paused and waited for an answer that as usual, was not forthcoming. "I mean, I can see how I ended up in his dream...sort of. He was dreaming about Dumbo and I was on an elephant so we sort of bumped into each other. But now I'm in my mom's dream. So how does Jojo stay with us?" She glanced at Tetta who glanced back while seeming distracted. *Are you downloading more info from the web?* Amelia thought at Tetta.

"I'm checking on availability." Tetta held up her hand asking Amelia to wait.

"Well?" Amelia was feeling anxious about what she might learn.

"Well?" Tetta repeated. "You humans never cease to amaze me. Yesterday you didn't even know information could be accessed in this manner, today it's not fast enough for you! Do I look like a Google search engine?"

Amelia blushed. "Sorry." Then she had another question. "Since you refer to me as human, are you something other than human?"

"Only humans see anything as *other than*," Tetta murmured. "I am One in the Same as you are. 'Human' is really only another word for form. At this moment I appear to you as having a human form, but you're dreaming right now, so you actually have no form to speak of and neither do I, and yet you think you see form. When you can explain that one to me we will continue this conversation."

Amelia wondered if she had insulted Tetta with her question, then she considered the delicate play on words Tetta had just employed, along with the new confusion they produced. "Sometimes I think

I'm better off not asking," she concluded.

"Watch your words," Tetta scolded.

Amelia waited to see what Tetta might tell her about Jojo. The questions had brought up several issues she had not considered before. How much time was elapsing while this dream was occurring? She had heard that most remembered dreams happen in the last few minutes before a person wakes up in the morning. Days had passed in this dream but perhaps it was only a matter of moments.

"Oh for goodness sake child!" Tetta finally interrupted Amelia's thoughts. "Does your thinking ever stop?"

"Oh! Shhh!" Amelia put her fingers to her lips then redirected them to her forehead tapping herself between the eyebrows. "Sorry." Her shoulders slumped and she focused her attention on the tip of her tongue as she lightly held it between her teeth trying to be quiet.

"It's okay." Tetta slowed the tempo of the conversation. "I just want you to practice the awareness that as you think so shall follow your experience. There's no sense exchanging one flawed belief system for another." Tetta reassured Amelia as she gently reached over and patted her hand. "That's what I mean by giving in to the flow. Just let it *Be*."

"I'm sorry, I seem to forget some things until you remind me of them."

"Few people learn things perfectly the first time child. Don't judge yourself." Tetta paused, then smiled. "PLEASE," she emphasized, "don't judge yourself!"

"Okay." Amelia smiled back. "So where are we?"

"I can tell you that you have a link to Jojo that is deeper than two dreams bumping into each other and this is what causes you to remain together. He is not here in the same way however. Jojo and Miguel both visit the waking dream daily while you remain in the Wait Zone."

"They wake up and then come back here?" Amelia clarified with

66

excited interest, realizing also that this meant her dream was indeed taking more than a few moments.

"When the pair disappears from your dream experience they are most likely visiting the waking dream."

"Miguel too? Do I also have a close tie to him?"

"Your words, not mine." Tetta clarified, "Miguel comes back to the dream you are presently sharing with many beings including myself and Hiram, even Binga." Tetta shrugged her shoulders. "Each player in any part of the dreamtime may have multiple relationships playing out during any sequence."

"Hiram? I've seen Hiram before?" Amelia asked.

"Oh for goodness sake child!" Tetta exclaimed. "What does it take to get you to see what you're seeing?"

"Do these relationships all go back to the waking dream?" Amelia asked.

"Not all. Some start in the Wait Zone."

"What's the Wait Zone?"

"Not important. That's more information than you need right now. It's a waiting room; no more, no less." Tetta tried to calm Amelia's fears.

"What am I waiting for?" It was too late. Amelia was beginning to imagine the worst.

"What every human waits for." Tetta was ready to stop the question and answer session. "A reason for being." She shook her head. "What a waste of time."

"It's a waste of time to want to find out why we exist and what we're supposed to do?" Amelia asked.

"You'd be doing it if you weren't so preoccupied with wondering what it was." Tetta waved her hands in the air almost as soon as the words left her mouth. "Not just you. Everyone. Almost all of humanity suffers the belief that they don't know what they're living for when, if they would just let go of their need to know — which is a failed effort to be safe, I might add — they would do better than *know*. They would *Be*." Amelia watched as Tetta stopped to scan the ethers.

"I can tell you this, my dear. You have never been one to search for the meaning of life. There is a long thread of avoiding knowledge, of ignoring facts and overlooking the unpleasant in your part of the web. For you, it is most important that you address this way of staying safe, again a fruitless endeavor, if you are ever to leave the Wait Zone."

Amelia stared at the guru turned granny. She could tell the audience was over. She felt a familiar sense of competition rise to the perceived threat that a failure to step up might cause her to lose her freedom. She grabbed her bottle of cola and walked over to the edge of the field where she could see Jojo and Hiram playing horseshoes. The boy was throwing the heavy U-shaped pieces of iron with skill and precision. Hiram would chuckle until he had to rest his hands on his knees to catch his breath. She was sharing her dream with him but she didn't know if he was also part of her waking life.

She imagined Miguel being in the waking life and wondered what sort of work he did, who his friends were, where he lived. *He could be from Spain.* Amelia laid down on the blanket and felt the sunlight sparkle through leaves to warm her skin. She wondered what drew Miguel to her dream and whether or not it was possible to visit this so-called Wait Zone while daydreaming.

As the shifting shapes of light and shadow moved across her closed eyelids, Amelia began to nod off in the warm summer breeze and found herself standing in the middle of heavy fog.

*Where am I? Where did everybody go?* Amelia wondered. The B-rated Halloween thriller anxiety began to mount. It occurred to her that she might have lost her dream connection with Tetta and the others. *I know, no others, everything's connected*, she nervously repeated her lesson with Tetta. Frantically, Amelia waved her hands in the air hoping it might clear. *I could be in trouble*, she thought. Then, thinking better of the manifesting qualities of that comment, she corrected herself, "No, I'm safe. I'm compleeeetly safe. In fact I don't even need to be safe at all. There isn't any such thing as unsafe. It's true. So true." Then, just for the heck of it she clicked her heels together and tried again, "There's no place like home. There's no place like home. There's no place like home... nothing."

Amelia tried calling Zeke but there was no answer. *Hrim?* she thought. Again, no reply.

"How 'bout me?" At the sound of a strange man's voice the fog parted and Amelia was looking at the horned manager that had appeared in her other dreams. Her eyes roll upward as her head wagged with distaste for the man and a frustrated groan filled her throat. "I'm always the last one you think about," he grumbled.

*There could be a very good reason for that!* Amelia thought, and then wondered what she meant by this statement that had come to mind so easily. Somehow the obvious interpretation she wasn't the type to hang out with horned devils seemed to come up short.

"I've been waiting and waiting for you to make up your mind and you still don't have a clue what you want." Amelia assessed the details of the horned manager in this dream. He was short on horns. However they were evident in his attitude. He wasn't wearing a black cape in this dream, but he did seem to be stuck on the same question that was in the first dream in the restaurant.

"These things take time," Amelia said, without knowing why. "I thought it would be okay to do two things at once."

"But now is not the time!" The man's voice turned anxious. He was pacing and looking out the window as if he were trying to find something. Amelia realized scenery was developing, but it wasn't coming with her thoughts. It was a part of his thoughts. She tried to sense what she was really feeling for the manager. She felt trapped, suffocated by his controlling manner. He was impatient and demanding and she felt conflicted about wanting to make some sort of a decision and also resistant to doing so because of the way he was pressuring her.

"I'm running out of time." He pointed low to the ground, shaking his finger and stomping his foot. "Just take those!" Amelia couldn't see a thing, but remained determined in her position.

"Nope, those are definitely not me." She replied as if she knew what he was talking about.

"No one's going to see them anyway." The man practically stomped his feet. His actions and intonation all suggested he thought Amelia was being ridiculous.

Amelia stood in shock and backed away from the man. "Shouldn't you above all people be most interested in this part?" she demanded.

"It's a simple decision." He moved toward her.

"Whether I'm a red state or a blue state?" Amelia recalled her options from the restaurant dream.

"How long are you going to criticize me for that? I thought it would be fun." The man's temperament turned to fury.

Amelia glared back. "It didn't fit, David!" she shouted feeling simultaneously angry and thrilled that she had remembered his name.

"It's not rocket science, Amelia. It's a simple decision."

"It all starts with this one decision," Amelia insisted.

"You're doing this backward!" David argued.

"I am not!" Amelia stomped her foot. "It all starts with the shoes and gold lame is not where I'm starting from!"

The sound of a record needle coming to a sudden stop screeched through her mind. Amelia jumped from the ground under the tree ready to finish her argument with David. She stood alone. Out in the field, the water balloon games had begun and she saw Jojo take a big one to his back. She looked around wildly. David the horned devil had disintegrated. She searched frantically through the crowd to locate Tetta. She was nowhere to be found. It became obvious this was something she alone needed to figure out.

*Pause, pause, pause...*

## The Other Side and the Other Other Side

Jahni led his group of 10 dreaming apprentices to the space between a pair of glowing pillars of light, and turned to address them.

"This is the Wait *Station*. It is the entry point to the Wait Zone." Jahni made the distinction between the two places for the small group of 10 students. "Those who cross over into the Wait Zone by way of transitioning out of the physical life are usually entertaining either the last few moments of their previous dream or the dream they expected to find once they crossed over."

Jahni scanned the group to see that each comprehended the meaning of his words. It was often possible that students still clung to their expectations of heaven, hell and other post-3-D eternal places long after they had witnessed the multi-dimensional realm of dreams. Having never been human, Jahni could not comprehend how it felt to believe that 3-D was real and everything else was imaginary except for a possible evergreen and peaceful heaven or fire-studded hell.

"In the Wait Zone you may help those in need reach the next level of consciousness. I must warn you, there are those who are dead *and* those who are still living in this place. Since this is your first visit I would like you to refrain from working with the still living as we don't wish to cross-over anyone who might not yet be ready."

"How can you tell the living from the dead?" one of the students asked.

"Those who are ready to go to the next level of consciousness will join you easily. You are not permitted to try to convince anyone they *should* cross over, understood?"

"What kind of living people are here?" asked another.

"Those in altered states of consciousness. Those who are on drugs, for example, can have experiences here." Jahni replied. "They may be very high on illegal or prescribed substances." Jahni thought of an example. "Acid, or morphine. Or they may be in a coma. This is why we're not going to work with the still living. Outside the Wait Zone are countless family and friends hoping their loved one will wake up."

"Are the brain-dead considered alive or dead here?" another student inquired. "I mean that's such a controversial issue."

"No matter what sort of testing can be done, humans will always resist ending a life. Death is what humans are most afraid of. Most humans don't understand how life continues or that it is concurrent in many frequencies at once." Jahni paused as a few students exchanged some quiet comments. "While 3-D is a very special experience with limited availability, and should be protected and preserved to get the most out of the experience, it is not all there is. What may help you is to know that if a person is brain-dead, they are among the dead here and may move on. If a person is not brain-dead, they are not dead here." The group murmured with additional discussion.

72

"Then, if we are not sure that a person is brain dead in 3-D we should not turn off life support, even if their body is incapable of supporting them." The student's question was more of a statement clearly charged with his own beliefs.

"Everyone dies from something. No one dies before his or her time." Jahni paused for murmuring tones that were both relieved and doubtful as many of the apprentices had gained interest in the other side after unexpectedly losing a loved one. "It is better if you explore this for yourselves. Move out, and I will meet you at the lift in a little while."

The group dispersed in pairs. The Wait Zone was an ever-changing scene based on the beliefs of the new arrivals. Smoldering fires and the echoes of protesting sufferers gave way to the delicate sounds of harp music flowing through pearly gates over golden streets. His students would enter these places as they dared to work with those who feared suffering their hellish dreams and escort those who had finally grown bored with their heavenly havens.

Jahni strolled toward the lift area where guides were surrounded by balls of light, misty figures, and what appeared to be glowing three-dimensional beings. All were variations of how humans believed they would appear in the so-called "next realm". They were about to learn just how many realms there were. Guides and groups were rising upward on cylinders of light lifting them into a sky that was so bright it was as if they were moving into the sun itself. Jahni smiled. It was his favorite ride.

As he walked he could hear a combination of sounds coming out of the fog of consciousness he was more or less ignoring. His least favorite aspect of the Wait Zone was the presence of drug addicts. They tended to be rude and invasive. As if his thoughts had invited the experience, a man walked out of the mist and started talking to Jahni.

73

"You think you're special?" Jahni eyed the man trying to determine how the man was seeing him. While his human students were free to choose whom they would help, as a guide, once he was engaged, Jahni was obliged to participate. The man reached out and leaned on Jahni.

"Don't do that," Jahni requested, pulling away from the man.

"Awwww, whatsamatter?" the man mocked with an ugly expression toward Jahni, "I could use a little support."

Turning, the man threw himself into an expensive winged back chair that appeared as he landed. The man stared as if he were mindlessly watching television. His eyes were red and his expression had turned to one of self-pity. His looks were neat and clean although his breath clearly indicated an extreme level of intoxication.

Jahni recognized that this man was different from the street junkies who showed up just as long as their highs lasted. While Guides are obliged to participate in the dreams of humans no matter how insane, they do not have to cooperate and there is no rule against obtaining additional information if they choose to be helpful. Jahni observed the man before him. While he was clearly drunk and there was no way to help him with reason, there was also something very needy about him. Something behind being wasted that Jahni wished to understand.

"Is there something I can do for you?"

"Yeah, get me a bottle of Brut."

"I'd rather not."

"Why not? Wha'd'you care?" The man's tone conveyed a sense of futility.

"Perhaps there's something else I could help you with? Something that might suit you better?" Jahni suggested.

"I am tired of not getting what I need because of someone else's agenda!" The drunken character complained.

Jahni scanned the man for data from the field and immediately bumped into a thread that ran straight to Hrim. He was surprised. *This guy is related to Hrim's project?* Jahni wondered. *I thought he quit chemical dependency a long time ago.* Jahni felt a little deeper into the field and saw a circle of people all extending threads toward one another with such frequency a web-like pattern developed. In addition to Hrim, Jahni saw Tetta was there too. Jahni looked down at the man sleeping in the chair.

*What are you doing here?* he thought.

*I'm waiting.* The man dreamed in response.

*For what?* Jahni asked.

*A chance to make it up to her,* the man replied in his sleep. *I can't help it, I love her.*

Jahni couldn't determine whom in the scene, including the drunk, could possibly be the one Hrim had described as undecided between living and dying. The possibilities tickled Jahni's love for working in the field, even if they were hinged on a drunk who was wasting his life. He loved the work he had learned to do as an apprentice of Hrim and suddenly longed for the chance to be back in the mix. He decided to visit Hrim to learn more about the case.

Looking up he saw one member of his students juggling a dozen balls of light that were all clamoring to get on the lift. He returned his gaze to the sleeping drunk. *I have to go now, sleep well, and consider learning a thing or two about moderation.* The drunk muttered something Jahni couldn't understand. *Thoughts are so much easier than slurred words,* he thought.

*Pause, pause, pause...*

Karen Bradford ran her hand through her dark hair and blinked in annoyance at the fluorescent light overhead. She never liked fluorescents. The buzz they made was irritating and their light was anything but natural. She knew the gray roots showing through her hair looked like hell in the light, but that really didn't matter right now. With as little sleep as she was getting, she knew she looked like hell in any light.

Putting her hand lightly on her daughter's hand she moved her fingers to the palm, away from the needles and tubes, and gently stroked the underside. She watched as a machine controlled her daughter's breathing. Her chest rose and dropped in an unnatural way. She searched her face for some sign her beautiful daughter was stirring back to awareness. But it did not appear she was about to open her eyes anytime soon.

Karen knew the doctors were waiting for her response. She wondered what kind of guessing game this was supposed to be. There was no way she could choose to shut it down. Her daughter was only 36 years old. *There's plenty of time,* she thought. *C'mon baby.*

The curtain around the bed moved and Karen recognized the nurse named Paul. "I need to take some readings." He waited for Karen to move away from the intravenous sacks hanging from a pole beside the bed.

"Alright, I need a stretch anyway." Karen gave her daughter's hand a squeeze and stood up. "I'll be right back, baby." She whispered to her daughter. For a moment she felt weak and stumbled one step backward. She smiled at Paul who reached toward her supportively. "I'm okay."

"Maybe you could use a break?" Paul suggested. "How about a little food, or sleep?"

"I just took a nap, but I will check the cafeteria for something." Karen agreed as she pulled back the curtain and walked out into the intensive care unit. She glanced back, "You know where to find me."

Turning around Karen nearly walked into a tall dark man who seemed to hover around Amelia's area on the unit more than anyone else.

"Can I help you?" she asked with the kind of sigh she had

adapted to indicate that the very sight of him was painful to her.

"Mrs. Bradford," he started.

"Please, this has gone on long enough and I'm tired of it." She waved her hand in his face. "Call me Karen."

"Karen," the man began again, "the doctors tell me there's no change." Amelia's mother bristled at the statement of the obvious.

"You never know what changes there might be, Detective. That shouldn't matter to your investigation anyway. All you have to do is get the person who did this."

"Ma'am, I know." Karen bristled again. She hated the word "ma'am" more than her daughter did.

"So why are you here?" She stomped her foot, then faltered as she took a step forward. Detective Alvarez reached his hand under her elbow and supported her long enough for her to regain her balance.

"Detective, I am exhausted." Karen forcefully pulled her elbow away from the detective's hand. "My daughter is not yet a murder victim and I don't intend to make her one. If you have anything positive to say, I suggest you do so."

"Can I buy you some dinner?" the detective quickly offered.

In the midst of all the rushing and visiting friends, meters going off and codes sounding on the unit, Karen Bradford felt isolated and alone. The curtain moved behind her and Paul stepped out.

"You're still here?" Paul asked tapping his pen on the clipboard.

"I have no where more important to be."

"You won't be here much longer if you don't get something to eat." Paul wagged the pen in the air.

"I just asked her to have some dinner with me," the detective volunteered again ducking down and trying to catch Karen's gaze.

"Okay, okay!" Karen covered her face and squeezed her head with her fingertips as if that could help her growing caffeine headache. "I'll eat!"

Detective Alvarez nudged gently on her elbow and Karen didn't pull away even though that would have been her usual instinct. Amelia's mother was proud of how tough she was. She was the helper, the one who was always there for someone else, always able to help.

Two days before she had just walked through the front door after a busy day of running last minute errands preparing for their trip when the call came. *Too late, I'm done for the day!* She had thought as she picked up the phone expecting to hear her daughter's voice making additional requests. Instead it had been Detective Alvarez advising her of the situation. She hadn't been home in a week. Neither of them had gotten onboard a plane that day, but the turbulence had never stopped.

Next to hospital chapels, hospital cafeterias are the most likely place to be empty. Karen Bradford had now visited them both. Karen hadn't felt safe in the dim darkness of the chapel and didn't feel hungry looking at the overly bright white reflective cafeteria. White tables reflected white fluorescent light. *Where is the ambiance?* Karen wondered.

Detective Alvarez steered Karen through the doors. She had been resisting eating anything, not just the cafeteria food. All she had taken the first 24 hours had been coffee to stay awake. She had given up coffee along with smoking, and had become a vegetarian all in the same month three years earlier, but one by one she feared her habits might change.

Karen looked apologizingly at the woman behind the glass case as she sneered at the vat of reconstituted powdered mashed potatoes. Meatloaf with gravy and green beans with ham came on to her tray next. She glanced behind her. Detective Alvarez wasn't pushing a tray.

"Excuse me, detective. But don't you think you ought to eat something too? After all you have to be strong to solve this mess."

The Detective stepped back and grabbed a tray. The caffeine headache pounded at Karen's head. It was amazing how quickly the addiction could come back. She looked at the meatloaf. *I'm still a vegetarian,* she thought, *I just happen to be eating meat right now.* Karen renewed her conviction to not smoke. She couldn't imagine how she could explain to Amelia that she had to smoke in order to survive the ordeal her daughter was experiencing. *No, that won't fly.*

While detective Alvarez paid for the meals Karen stood looking at the empty room filled with tables. For a moment she felt like she did on the last day of school when the children had left. There was always the thrill of summer vacation and the melancholy of knowing she wouldn't see certain children again.

This summer had been different. Though the circumstances of taking the trip were unfortunate for Amelia, Karen had been thrilled with the prospect of going to India with her daughter. It was something she had never dreamed possible and a memory she looked forward to making.

Detective Alvarez stepped up next to Karen and then nodded toward a table as if he were seating her in a busy restaurant. "This way?" he motioned with his tray. She followed. The pair sat their trays on the table and put themselves in the uncomfortable orange bowl-shaped chairs. Karen obligingly picked up her fork and toyed with her mashed potatoes as she picked up her coffee and drank it black. She had always been a sugar and cream coffee drinker. Not giving herself the sweet and enriching additives was almost a decision in line with her present level of hardship. She was determined not to enjoy anything until she could do so with her daughter.

"Is there anything you can tell me about your daughter that might help me with my investigation?" Detective Alvarez asked a question Karen was certain he had asked before.

"What do you want me to say?" she asked. "This is something that would absolutely never happen to my daughter." Karen felt herself turning emotional and blinked the tears back. She took a deep breath and another sip of the still too hot coffee.

"I just thought you've had a little time to think and something might have occurred to you," the detective clarified.

"What is occurring to me is that you haven't got a clue!"

"No, I don't." Detective Alvarez apologized.

Karen glared at the food sitting on both their plates. "We need to eat."

"Yes, of course."

Pressing his fork sideways into overly crisp fried fish, Detective Alvarez chopped it into bite size pieces. Karen watched for a moment and comforted herself with the memory of the dream from her nap at her daughter's bedside. She looked at the detective who was, for all appearances, as tired and hungry as she was. She regretted the resistance she had expressed toward him and simultaneously was glad for someone who seemed patient enough to withstand it.

"She's going to be okay," she told him, remembering the words Amelia had said in the dream. "She's coming home soon."

The detective looked deeply into her eyes and smiled reassuringly. "Yes, of course."

*Pause, pause, pause...*

Amelia watched in a daze as Jojo was chosen by the captain of one of the softball teams that was forming. Hiram walked out to the mound and took up his position as pitcher.

"Tell me." Amelia turned to see Tetta approaching.

"What?" Amelia asked, not yet fully cognizant of the futility of pretending she wasn't thinking about her dream.

"Your dream is very important. What do you think it means?"

"Means?"

"Yes, dreams are very often symbolic of events that may seem

80

unrelated."

Amelia was distracted as Jojo came up to bat. The ball crossed the plate and the boy did not swing. "Steee-rike One!" the umpire called out.

*Watch the first one,* Amelia heard a voice in her head say as she saw the boy gauge the pitch for his next shot at the ball. She turned her attention back to Tetta's question.

"I was in a shoe store," Amelia remembered. "I was with this man who has been elsewhere in my dreams. Usually he has horns but not this time."

Amelia watched as Jojo swung hard, connecting with the next pitch and started to run for first base before he dropped the bat.

"I was arguing with him about the shoes." Amelia glanced down. The very same gold lamé shoes were there on her feet. "He told me I was shopping all wrong."

Amelia noticed Jojo was heading for second as the ball was tossed to a nearby player. *Hold up! Hold up!* Amelia thought. Jojo waited as if he could hear her.

"I told him it all starts with the shoes."

Tetta laughed. "It is easier to find the clothes to go with the shoes than the shoes to go with the clothes," she agreed.

"But that's just it Tetta. I don't know how, but I'm certain that I would never buy these shoes, let alone wear the clothes that go with them. Not by choice anyway!" Amelia was adamant.

"Never?"

"No. These are something someone would wear to a bad wedding." Amelia stopped. Something clicked into place and just that quickly clicked out of place.

The next player swung and barely moved the ball. Jojo raced to steal third as Hiram jogged in toward the catcher to help retrieve the ball.

"Wedding." Amelia's mind clicked again. "His name was David."

"Whose?"

"The horny man's name was David." Amelia's jaw dropped and she stared at Tetta in wide-eyed amazement. "I think I was going to marry him."

"You would buy shoes you hated for your own wedding to a man with horns?" Tetta sounded doubtful.

"No." Amelia searched her non-existent memory.

"*He* wanted me to buy them."

"So this David character," Tetta asked, "he liked gold lamé shoes?"

"No. He was anxious about something, like we didn't have the time to be messing around over the shoes. He was pushing me to get something – anything – so we could leave the store."

"What do you think was making him so nervous?"

"I don't know. He just kept looking out the window like we needed to get someplace." Amelia remembered the ease with which the horny manager watched her start to leave in her theatre dream. "… or he wanted me to leave."

"What then?"

"I don't know."

"Oh, never say 'I don't know' when remembering a dream. You lock it out."

"Oh." Amelia was sure she didn't remember anything else.

"Did you buy the shoes?" Tetta asked.

"I must have." Amelia looked down at her feet.

The crowd cheered and Amelia looked up as Jojo approached home plate along side the softball. "Slide!" she yelled. Jojo hit the ground. His leg crossed the plate before the ball touched him. Jojo was on his feet jumping up and down with his arms held victoriously in the air.

*Pause, pause, pause…*

*Consciousness permeates all things. Within the various frequencies of creation, countless layers of consciousness may be accessed and utilized. This holographic environment is what produced most of the three dimensional experiences humans have today.*

*Human beings tend to explore probability-generating fields of consciousness arriving at both expected and unexpected outcomes. Combined results of group consciousness have forged little grooves in the stuff that dreams are made of which direct imaginations along popular courses of action.*

*Those who come to the realization that they can depart from predetermined pathways to create their own new roads often become track jumpers. They can see the storyline they are experiencing and choose a different one. Others become so experienced at making these choices they are no longer subject to the conditions of predetermined consciousness and can move about the planes of existence at will without reason or provocation.*

*Most achieve this only by going into service to others. This is quite simply because those who maintain personal agendas are egotistically attached to particular conditions and are unable to take leave of these senses.*

*The prevailing stories of Beta and Alpha awareness appear to be what humans are most attached to due to their 3-dimensional outcomes. Being able to move from these brain wave states to Theta and deeper Delta vibrations while maintaining lucidity is fully appreciated only after an individual has moved beyond the limitations of waking consciousness. At these levels explorers may consciously work directly with creative energy, rather than confusing their identities with its physical outcomes.*

*Resume, resume, resume...*

Jahni never connected with Alpha or Beta awareness. His entire career had been spent in Delta frequencies and beyond. The encounter with the stoner in the Wait Zone brought Jahni to a curious dalliance with Theta waves and the possibility of a little vacation into the karmic realms.

Masterful at inter-dimensional travel and thrilled to have an excuse to closely explore connections with the physical plane, Jahni connected with the energy that he knew as Hrim and found himself walking out of a wooded area into a field. His clothing had shifted from white robe to khaki slacks, sport shirt and leather loafers. It took him only a moment to spot Hrim and catch up with him.

*Well now, what brings you this way?* Hrim was surprised to see Jahni outside the University and the Wait Zone. Jahni scanned Hrim and found his character to be named Hiram. He also found that the woman could hear think-speak so he fell into character and used spoken words to cover his tracks.

"I just left the fields and thought I'd share some interesting news with you." Jahni nodded to Jojo and Miguel as he slowed down. Hrim stopped to talk with him. "There's a pretty drunk fellow in the receiving area that seems to be attached to you and your crew. I wasn't sure if you had a chance to venture over there lately. I've seen him two or three times. He's adamant about making up with a woman he loves. Do you know of whom I'm talking? Who is your undecided case?"

Hrim looked at the group moving across the field. "To tell you the truth Jahni, except for Tetta, every one of them is up in the air right now." Jahni looked at the man who was walking with his hand on the shoulder of the boy who was taking a snail from the woman.

"All three of them?" Jahni considered the possibilities that could take three lives at once and guessed, "Car accident?"

"Separate incidents, same reason," Hrim informed him.

"That's a lot to cover."

"Yes, Tetta is helping me to handle the shifting scenery. All three are active in multiple dreams. The boy, Jojo, as is the case with kids, adds a lot of diversity to the dreamtime."

"What about the man?" Jahni asked.

"Miguel? Not figuring in just yet but he could go lucid at any moment."

"So the character back at the Wait Zone, his dream isn't figuring in yet either?"

"Not yet. Popping in and out," Hrim verified.

"So there's no one else?"

"Oh yeah, there's a whole team of characters that are bouncing around Amelia's dreams right now."

Jahni looked at Amelia recognizing that she had the key. "Shoes?"

"Yep."

"Isn't that a little..." Hrim beat Jahni to the punch.

"Ruby slipper?"

"Yeah. So...movie musical ago."

"Um-hmm," Hrim continued the metaphor, "but the wicked witch might be winning and this man behind the curtain isn't sure who or what could come up next."

"I've got an idea," Jahni offered.

"You don't need to dance around the subject Jahni, I would be grateful if you could lend a hand."

The pair started walking again, and Hrim prepared to introduce Jahni to the crew. "Fried chicken and potato salad!" Jahni observed, "I think I just died and went to heaven!" They laughed.

Hrim and Jahni joined the dinner table with full plates and empty stomachs. "Everyone, this is Johnny, my brother from Darke County," Hrim introduced. "He's come to visit for the weekend."

"Wonderful." Tetta smiled at Jahni in warm recognition. "Are you going to stay long enough to visit the circus with us tomorrow?"

"I wouldn't miss it for the world!" Jahni was shaking hands with Miguel and rubbed Jojo's head. "I'm going to pick up a little good luck from you mister. Those were some great plays you made out there!"

"Thanks!" Jojo beamed holding Dumbo up for Jahni's inspection. "This is Dumbo, he's my lucky snail!"

"Did he teach you how to slide like that?" Jahni asked.

"No, I listened to my coach." He smiled at Amelia. She smiled back, only slightly distracted by the appearance of Johnny and a continuing feeling that something about Hiram was familiar to her.

The picnic was followed by a show of fireworks that lit up the clear evening sky. Families lay on their blankets in the field and greeted their favorites with "ooohs" and "aaaahs". Amelia studied the faces of her newfound friends as the flashing fireworks shined different colors on their faces. Jojo was completely entranced as he leaned his back against Miguel's chest. Hiram, Johnny and Tetta sipped cider as they watched. Afterward, families walking home found their way lit by fireflies.

The configuration of people Amelia walked with wasn't really her family and she wondered if the other groups walking down the road were really families. Her mother's dream had attracted the consciousness of hundreds of participants who had bumped into it and made it quite a celebration. She wondered if the connecting theme that brought them all together was the Fourth of July, picnics, ball games, or possibly family reunions.

Amelia found comfort in the way everything worked in the dreamtime. No one seemed to need a special reason to be with someone else. Everyone was, as Tetta said, *One*. What she didn't see was that some people did have a special reason to be with someone else and for one person in particular, that reason wasn't exactly small town pure.

From a distance their group seemed like all the others, but the discerning eye, the eye of one who had something to lose, something he was unwilling to give up, that eye saw danger in the well being of this little group.

*I never meant to hurt you. But now, what can I do?* A shadowy figure moved behind the tree to keep the group in sight.

Jahni stopped. His attention was grabbed from the group and he turned his head to find a visual for the sound of the voice he heard in his mind. It was directed straight at them. Hrim and Tetta noticed the departure of his attention from the friendly dream scene but they hadn't heard the voice.

"What's going on?" Miguel turned to ask. The three quickly composed themselves. The prospect of danger was a sure trigger for Miguel. There were already three guides working on this project. They didn't need any heroes trying to take over, but it was too late.

Miguel scanned the surroundings and saw what the threesome had been looking for. While they tried to distract him, Miguel watched the figure of a single man moving from behind a nearby tree and disappearing around the corner of a house. *Crime lurks on the streets of Main Street America?* Miguel thought. He knew it was true. There was no place in the country where the effects of drugs and even gangs hadn't warped the scenery. Still he found something eerie in this incident. It didn't have the feel of a random street crime. He didn't anticipate the group was about to be mugged. There was something more ominous surrounding the encounter. He couldn't quite put his finger on the feeling of meeting with destiny. He scanned the faces of Johnny, Hiram, and Tetta. They had returned to socializing as if nothing had happened.

Miguel didn't know what had caught their attention, but he stayed toward the back of the group now, watching, to see if he could get a better view of this man. His hand automatically went to the side of his ribs under his right arm. Becoming aware that he was reaching he realized he was looking for a holster. Seeing that, the full memory of being a detective entered into his awareness and he realized that he was dreaming.

Hiram turned to say something to Tetta then allowed himself to slow down and join Miguel at the back of the pack. Miguel could see that Hiram was concerned about his growing awareness and so decided not to share what he was experiencing with him. There was something out of place. Tetta, Hiram and Johnny had a different feel to him than Amelia and Jojo. He felt certain protectiveness toward the boy and Amelia and a strange detachment for Hiram and Johnny. He felt he had met Tetta under some other circumstances but couldn't place her.

Hrim listened to Miguel's thoughts. It was obvious he had a breakthrough but gratefully, did not have all the details. The holster had not appeared. Miguel was too confused, by his own standards, to be carrying a weapon. Hrim determined that Miguel was neither going to act out of character for the moment nor share his insights with anyone else. Miguel could possibly become high maintenance now, but sometimes the things that moved dreams along weren't always predictable.

The three guides would have to be more careful now to not interfere with the unfolding of events that would bring the dream to its conclusion. At the same time they were responsible for seeing to it that no one crossed over before his or her time.

Engrossed with determining the effects new awareness would bring to the scene, no one noticed that the shadowy figure had not exited the scene for long. From the corner of another house he watched Miguel carefully to determine if he had been seen. It didn't seem anything had changed. The group seemed as comfortable and calm as before.

A streak of panic combined with frustration ran through the very soul of the dark figure. Still thinking in 3-D terms, he was sure that his power would be curbed or accelerated by the interference or compliance of others. The dream world was not new to him. He was experienced in functioning in altered states of consciousness without seeming as if anything was different about him. What he wasn't sure of was how to accomplish what he needed to do in a way that would be effective without a doubt.

*Pause, pause, pause...*

"When we go to the circus tomorrow can I get some cotton candy?" Jojo peered up into Tetta's face as they walked side by side. "Not too much," Tetta mused. Jojo pulled in front of Amelia walking backward facing her.

"When we go to the circus tomorrow can we see the clowns?"

"Of course," she replied smiling. Jojo started running back and forth across the sidewalk with his arms raised in the air.

"When we go to the circus tomorrow can we watch the acrobats?"

"Sounds like a plan." Hiram nodded.

The group climbed the steps to the front porch.

"Can I fly off a trapeze?"

"No!" Everyone shouted. The group gathered in the kitchen to discuss the plans for the circus. They continued to answer Jojo as he asked one question after another with lightening speed. Amelia was impressed with his ability to think and speak without a break.

"I think I'm going to turn in. It looks like tomorrow is going to be a very busy day!" After a series of good night and sweet dreams well wishes, Amelia excused herself from the gathering and went to her room.

All of the conversations of the day ran through her mind as she changed into her flannel pajamas and crawled into the double bed beneath the big down comforter. *We must be in a town up North,* she thought. *It gets pretty cold here at night.*

Amelia wriggled out from under the comforter and pulled the big window closed, automatically locking it as she did so. She noticed the reflex and decided she must come from the city as she snuggled back under the comforter.

Outside the man waiting in the shadows of the bushes wasn't ready to give up. He moved around the corner of the house and pulled himself up by the window ledge to look through the next window. He watched as Miguel read a story to Jojo and tucked him into bed. The man outside the window was filled with frustration at the homey sight. Miguel ran his hand over Jojo's head and switched off the light as he left the room and closed the door. The man outside the window let his weight slide down the side of the house. The task that was ahead of him was complicated. If he had to make a move he had to take them all together or one of the others might be able to identify him. He emerged from the bushes on the side of the house and started heading away from town.

*Pause, pause, pause...*

# 5

## *Clowning Around*

"The circus is coming to town!" Jojo shouted as he ran through the front door, through the house, out the backdoor traveling the wrap-around porch to reach the front door again. "Come one, come all to the Big Top today!" Jojo sprinted across the living room floor and leapt into a handstand next to the piano in the dining room. Amelia, Tetta and Miguel applauded his calisthenics.

"Are you ready?" Jojo begged breathlessly wearing a proud smile. "Can we go now?"

"I thought we'd have breakfast at the diner," Tetta offered.

"That sounds like fun," Amelia agreed.

"Good, I'll call Hiram and invite him and Johnny to join us there." She smiled at Miguel, "Do you think you could convince Jojo that his Superhero pajamas are not appropriate attire even for a circus?"

Miguel put his hand on Jojo's jumping shoulder, "Come on little guy, let's get you dressed for whatever adventures there may be today." The two exited the room. Amelia wondered if it was time for them to go into waking life.

"No, no dear. This is clearly dreamtime." Amelia smiled at Tetta who was humming while doing nothing in particular.

"Whose dreamtime?" Amelia asked.

"Why, we're all visiting Jojo's dream now."

"Funny," Amelia noticed, "Jojo's dream looks a lot like my mother's."

"Ahh," Tetta smiled, "that's the joy of dreams. They weave together so many different possibilities without any seeming conflict." The old woman arranged herself on the rocker. This morning she wore a red and white checked blouse and dark blue jeans. Amelia felt uncomfortable looking down at Tetta so she sat next to the rocker on the floor.

"Let me give you a little Upanishad." Tetta went into a way of speaking that Amelia was beginning to recognize as giving lessons.

"Upanishad?" Amelia repeated.

"As in to take a lesson from the foot of the master." Tetta tapped her shoes on the floor.

"Are you a master?" Amelia asked.

"I am a very old woman. Ancient, you might say. How many old people do you know who don't think they have the answers?" Amelia smiled at Tetta. She never really thought of it like that. She watched as Tetta's eyes softened.

"Humans don't realize that the stuff of dreams is endless. There is never 'not enough'. Humans use the plenty to create the limits of their dreams. Do you see?" Tetta's head rolled back as if she was breathing in some sort of knowledge. "You are having a dream, and your mother is having a dream, and Jojo is having a dream, and Miguel is having a dream. Lots of people are having lots of dreams. Your dream intersects with Jojo's dream and so you become a *part* of one another's dreams. You think Jojo is your friend. Someone you know. It is exactly that. You know Jojo inside your own dream. Yet Jojo may not know himself the same way in his own dream. Because you are connected to your mother's dream, everyone who knows you knows your version of her dream through you. They like this part of the dream and so adapt that dream for themselves too. Jojo adds some of his own stuff to the dream, like the circus. He saw it coming, and he will produce it and because we are all connected to Jojo's dream we will go along with it and maybe add some of our own to it. This is collective dreaming. So the dream you think looks like your mother's dream is actually a collective dream. You have added your dream to it, so has Miguel, and others. It is constantly shifting shape. It is the same with the dream of the planet and all of your waking dreams. The only thing different in the waking dream is the belief that it's not a dream at all."

Amelia was anxious to ask questions throughout Tetta's teaching yet managed to wait, hoping it would all make sense when she was through. "So, when I met Hrim whose dream was that? Mine or Jojo's?"

"Yes." Tetta shrugged her shoulders and giggled.

"We were both dreaming of Hrim?" Amelia almost scowled at Tetta's playfulness.

"And Hrim was dreaming of you."

"One person sucked us both into his dream?"

"The elephant was a common denominator," Tetta advanced.

"So Hrim came because both Jojo and I had an elephant in mind at the time? I don't remember thinking anything about an elephant." Amelia searched her memory of her encounter with Hrim in the fog.

"For Jojo it was the elephant. For you," Tetta closed her eyes, tipped her head back and searched the field to check for boundaries, "... for you, it was India."

"India?" Amelia remembered Hrim asking her if she had always wanted to take a safari just after the rainforest appeared. "But why was it important that Jojo's dream and my dream were connected by this one elephant?" Amelia asked.

"It didn't have to be an elephant but it was the first common denominator that also carried meaning."

"Then someone or something else could have appeared other than Hrim?"

"No, Hrim could have appeared as someone or something else."

"Hrim can change what he looks like?" Amelia put this information together with the morphing figure she watched in the documentary and tried to remember what had been said about that. Then she remembered how the tiger turned into a man just before he dropped off the path to the village. Forgetting about the documentary, Amelia pursued learning more about which dreams belonged to whom. "That part of the dream, when we were on the mountainside and Jojo had a little battle with the tiger," Amelia went on, "that was more Jojo's dream than mine, correct?"

"Yes, Jojo's imagination took center stage. This is so important to the 3-D life, this factor of taking on someone else's dreams. If you could see all the times you take someone else's dream personally and make it seem like your own. When you do this and it isn't really your dream you give your energy to it but you can't change it because it isn't yours to change. The only thing you can do is let it go."

Amelia's attention turned to the dream of the horny manager. "I made his dream my dream didn't I? I took on his anxiety. That's why we fought. We were both fighting for our own dreams to be center stage as if one dream might cancel out the other." Tetta looked but did not answer Amelia. It was as if she was waiting for more. Amelia could tell that this was another moment when it was up to her alone to perceive what was next. She struggled to hold on to her train of thought. The train had left the station and she still wasn't sure where it was going.

*Pause, pause, pause...*

Jojo slid to Tetta's feet at the base of the rocking chair. "I'm ready to go!" The youngster was filled with more energy than his body could contain.

"Good for you! I think we should go to town and get a big stack of hotcakes and bacon to start us off right!" Tetta stood and looked at Amelia. "He's on first, you're on deck."

"Where's Miguel?" Amelia asked

"On third." Tetta continued the ballgame analogy to decipher whose dream was where for Amelia. "He went ahead. He said he'd meet us there." Tetta headed for the front door.

"Did you call Hiram and Johnny?" Jojo asked.

"Oh dear I almost forgot." Tetta turned and picked up the phone receiver from the table next to the rocking chair. Amelia looked at it. With its cord that ran to the phone and the pedestal table beneath, it reminded her of the table in her dream where the horned manager had not allowed her to take a call. She glanced down at the gold lamé shoes and wondered once again about her relationship to this man, the way he needed to control her, and the possibility that she might marry someone like that. *Horny manager,* she thought, *that seems to be a pretty good metaphor for a controlling boyfriend.*

"Miss Amelia, we're going!" Jojo shouted from the porch. Amelia jumped into action.

"I'm with you!" She joined him on the porch and pulled the door shut behind her.

The town was alive with Saturday morning business. Trucks were parked at the Hardware and Feed store loading wood and tools for weekend projects. The barbershop had a healthy crowd of men telling jokes and laughing, and Miguel was among them. The diner had a waiting line. Amelia joined the line behind Tetta while Jojo scouted out other kids with whom he could share his excitement about the circus.

Amelia watched Miguel across the street but was thinking about Hrim. *If he wasn't an elephant, what was he?* She looked at Tetta. *Is Hrim like you? Are you a real woman?*

Tetta smiled at Amelia. *You do have a lot of thoughts going on today don't you?* She reached her hand into the air and waved to Hiram and Johnny. "Hello!" The two joined them in line. "Miguel!" Tetta waved to the group across the street. "Come along, we're going in!" Miguel waved good-bye to the other men he was speaking with, and jogged across the street.

When Amelia entered the diner she could hardly believe her eyes. It was her dream. It was the restaurant she had been in when she first realized something was wrong. Her eyes darted to the corner across the room, but the horned manager was not there. Quickly images from her very first dream sequence flew through her mind. There was no Rumba line of people with masks and capes, no Jackie Gleason type or Judy Garland whispering in her ear.

"Are you alright dear?" Tetta gently put her hand on Amelia's forearm. Amelia barely felt it. She felt very far away from everything. *How can my dream be in Jojo's dream?* she wondered.

*Anyone can bring anything to the dream as long as it doesn't cross Jojo's boundaries,* Tetta replied.

*So I'm causing this?* Amelia asked.

*Not exactly causing it, Dear, no, but you require it.*

*What do you mean I require it?*

*There is something in this scene for you if you have eyes to see. There is something about this place that may help you remember what you need to know.*

*Did you make this place come back?* Amelia felt angry. She wanted answers not riddles.

*If I could access the information you need I would tell you outright. The opportunity came up for this place to manifest and as the scene still holds a charge for you, here we are.*

*What opportunity?* Amelia asked simultaneously realizing it was

96

Tetta's request of Jojo that they eat breakfast at the Diner. *You made room for this to happen then?* she clarified.

*Yes, but to help, not to harm. Please Amelia, don't waste your time here being upset. See what might spark your memory instead.*

Amelia considered her relationship to Tetta. She could not for the life of her understand what had drawn this woman into her life or why she should trust her at all. Yet given the situation she was in she didn't feel she had much of a choice. She was learning from Tetta; she just hoped what the old woman was teaching was true.

Amelia shook her shoulder length curly red hair back from her face and walked to the booth with Tetta. It was a large booth that held six people. Amelia was given a spot on the outside edge. Miguel sat on the other side of Tetta from her in the same seat. Jojo was seated directly across the table from Amelia with Hiram next and Johnny seated in the corner farthest from Amelia.

Amelia looked at Johnny and then at Hiram. Something seemed to be wrong. Something about the two brothers just didn't fit. They didn't look alike but might when Johnny was as old as Hiram. Amelia's eyes darted back and forth between the pair. Hiram was old enough to be Johnny's grandfather.

"Do you two come from a large family?" Amelia asked settling her eyes on Hiram.

"Me and Johnny?" Hiram asked. "No, just the two of us."

"Where are you from?" Amelia was proceeding with a little sleuthing.

"Small town nearby called Richmond." Hiram's eyes twinkled.

"Were your parents from there as well?" Amelia thought she would catch him with this one but Hiram was well aware of her thought process.

"My mother was from Fort Loramie," Hiram responded

"And my mom was from Richmond," Johnny jumped into the conversation.

"Same dad," Hiram finished.

Amelia was disappointed. It was entirely possible that Johnny's mother was far younger than Hiram's and able to bear children long into their father's old age. She felt a nudge from Tetta. *Move on dear, this conversation can happen anywhere. What do you remember about this place?* Tetta urged.

The waiter approached the table and fixed his eyes on Amelia. "Have you come to a decision?" he asked. Amelia hadn't even considered what she would have for breakfast. She glanced down at the menu. It was a dinner menu and a pricey one at that. No appetizer was under $20. No entrée was below $36.

"Something to drink?" the waiter asked. Amelia was dumbfounded by the selection of exotic foods on the menu. "Ma'am?"

"Water with lemon," Amelia blurted out. The waiter departed as if there was no one else at the table. Amelia looked around. She was the only one in the booth.

Fear gripped at Amelia's throat and chest. Suddenly she couldn't say anything. She couldn't swallow. She couldn't feel her feet. She peered over her knees toward the gold lamé shoes. She felt strangely safe as long as they were on. *More Dorothy in Oz,* she thought.

Amelia looked around the room for anything that might serve as a clue, a connection with whatever she needed to know. Directly behind her, a couple that seemed more consistent with small town diner than upscale restaurant were holding hands across the table. At the table for two beside her booth a woman dressed in black daintily checked her Palm pilot while she waited. What she was seeing wasn't making sense, as it hadn't the first time she had the dream.

*I'm in an expensive restaurant,* Amelia reminded herself. *That could be a symbol of... what?*

"I'm glad you could make it." David, sans horns, was seating himself across the booth from Amelia. His Gucci suit was creased razor sharp as if he had just put it on. Despite his improved attire compared to the mismatched shorts and sport shirt he wore at the shoe store, David remained edgy and seemed uncomfortable. "I want to apologize."

Amelia could only imagine that their previous argument had ended in a terrible squabble. She felt her fingers wrap around something on her finger.

"I don't want an apology David," she found herself saying. David smiled weakly. "I don't want dinner either." David's smile fell away from his face. "I only came to give you this." Amelia locked on to the ring just below the oversized diamond. She pulled it off and held it out across the table.

"Mimi," David's eyes pleaded into hers, "you can't mean this."

"I do," she insisted, setting the ring on the table. "I mean I can't David. I can't marry you."

David looked at the ring with astonishment, as if he had just spied a cockroach in his salad. Several seconds passed by. He didn't say or think anything Amelia could grasp.

*What are you thinking?* Amelia thought.

*This can't be happening!* he seemed to reply.

"Why are you so surprised?" Amelia began to realize she was reliving a conversation which had already taken place. "We haven't been getting along for months. This needed to end."

"But Mimi," David recited his lines, "what about all of our plans? We've paid for everything in full."

"I have paid for everything in full," Amelia corrected, and then wondered, *I did?*

"Well, of course you did, but it was for us!" an exasperated David insisted, and then defended, "and things are going to turn around for me you know." He pulled nervously on the sleeves of his jacket.

"I'm sorry David. I'm leaving." Amelia began to stand. She saw his hands shooting across the table and felt them landing on her shoulders.

"No!" He pushed and Amelia fell back on the seat. She looked around the room. It was as if no one had noticed the use of physical force. David's face was red. "I'm afraid that's not possible." David stared at the table trying to compose himself, his face becoming more and more red.

"I don't think you get to decide that for me anymore." Amelia stood again and braced herself for some sort of resistance from David or any other person present.

"Amelia," David leapt out of the booth and went after her as she headed for the door, "you can't leave like this. Look at the state you're in!" He looked at her as though she was upset.

*I'm not in any state! Amelia* thought. She could feel her teeth gritting together. "You really need to get some help David, and it isn't going to come out of my purse anymore." Amelia pushed past David and went through the door rummaging through her purse. She grabbed a ticket and held it up for the Valet.

"Thanks!" Jojo chimed as he took Dumbo's clear container from between her fingers.

Amelia looked up incredulously. Tetta and Hiram flanked her on either side while Miguel leaned on a parking meter and conversed with Johnny a few feet away.

*How did it go Amelia?* Tetta's voice sounded softly in her head.

*Better than last time.* Amelia shook her head. *Sort of.*

Jojo was on fire with anticipation. "There's going to be amazing acrobats!" he declared, "and tremendous trainers of lions, tigers, and bears!"

"Oh my!" Amelia couldn't resist another play on the Oz theme. She was amused at the way the story continued to play as a metaphor in the dream. As the group made their way toward the circus tents she checked her story against Dorothy's famous adventure.

*Let's see,* she thought, *innocent little girl finds herself lost with her dog in a strange world filled with people, some who want to help her and some who want to hurt her.* She didn't think there was anyone in her dream who meant her any harm.

She looked at Jojo dancing in front of Hiram enumerating the descriptions of the circus entertainers listed on the commemorative poster he got at the gate.

*Munchkin,* Amelia thought.

"Where to first?" Miguel asked as he returned with a huge glob of cotton candy on a paper cone for Jojo. As Jojo pulled off a piece and put it in his mouth Amelia could almost see the cavities developing in his teeth. *Clearly,* she thought, *this is totally his dream. Then she wondered at her concern for his dental health. Perhaps I'm a dentist,* she wondered. *Maybe that's how I became rich enough to support a boy toy like David.*

Trouble was, as far as she was concerned, David wasn't much of a toy. She considered the possibility that maybe there had once been some level of likeable personality about him. She thought perhaps he had come upon hard times and how much it could have hurt him when she pulled out the safety net. She wondered how David figured into her being stuck in the dream state.

Amelia looked down at her feet. She couldn't remember if she had been wearing the gold lamé shoes in her dream. *How do these damn things figure in?* The best guess she had on the whole scene was that she had broken up with David having finally realized how incompatible they were after a fight about shoes.

"Elephants it is!" Miguel announced as if he were Jojo's personal commentator for the day. His interest in Jojo was budding, or Jojo was dreaming himself a veritable father figure.

"Hey Miss Amelia," Jojo called, "we're gonna' go find Hrim!" Amelia smiled. She wondered if the elephant, their common denominator, might show up at the circus after all.

*Pause, pause, pause...*

The big top was smaller than the larger circuses Miguel had seen at the arena downtown when he was a kid. There was no tent in the big circus. Walking through the entrance with Jojo, he felt like a kid

101

again. He felt almost compelled, as Jojo was, to run in search of a front row seat. The handbill indicated there was an elephant that could dance and another that could do headstands.

Jojo found a long bench in the stands that would seat all six in their party. "The clowns are in here, too, with the elephants, and after that comes the wild animal trainers!" Miguel laughed as Jojo could barely squeeze the words through his heavy-breathing, all-too-excited body. He looked at Tetta, Johnny, and Hiram talking quietly among themselves and felt a pang of concern cross his thoughts. Something seemed to be going on in the background beneath all of the excitement and thrills for Jojo.

Jahni noticed Miguel's thoughts out of the corner of his mind and scanned for awareness. "He doesn't remember going lucid last night," Hrim confirmed. "I checked him out in the waking dream."

"Smart," Jahni acknowledged. "Have you locked on to the drunk in the Wait Station too?"

"He wasn't there last night," Hrim replied, "I could be off sequence."

"Hard to tell when someone's using," Tetta agreed. "So what are we looking for here?"

"My guess is an opportunity for some heroics and perhaps a little leveling of the playing field," Hrim offered. "I paid a visit to Jojo's home base last night and the picture wasn't very pretty."

Tetta looked at the boy jumping out of his chair to check on the arrival of the elephants. He seemed so happy while at the same time finding it difficult to stay still when he was looking forward to something. "How can we help?" she asked.

"Well, Jojo is pretty talented in the dream state," Hrim informed Jahni and Tetta. "He has already taken on his stepfather whether he appeared as a man or a tiger."

"The boy has no fear?" Jahni asked.

"The boy has a lot of fear, and it's affecting him pretty badly in every area of his life," Hrim corrected. "He has difficulty in school and isn't exactly viewed as a team player, so he doesn't play sports or have any other outlet. When he dreams he can turn the tables and be effective over his circumstances," Hrim added. "But when he's awake he is more likely to hide in his room with his snail."

"So we anticipate more heroics on his part this evening?" Jahni asked.

"Probably the boy will try to prove himself a man again." Hrim sighed. "Unfortunately, there's no getting through to his stepfather."

"Well, Jojo can let off some steam trying!" Jahni offered.

"As long as no one gets hurt," Tetta replied.

"Now, Tetta." Hrim put his hand around her shoulder.

"I know, I know." She squeezed his hand.

*Pause, pause, pause...*

*Bodhisattvas are enlightened beings who choose to not cross over into Nirvana, even when they have earned the privilege. They have become so good they wish to help the rest of humanity do the same before they retire to spend eternity in bliss.*

Resume, resume, resume...

Tetta was not exactly a bodhisattva, but she was also not an etheric guide. She could not shape shift the way Hrim could, yet she also didn't return to waking life after sleeping. Tetta's specialty was working with the Undecided, yet she leaned toward sending them back to the 3-D world whenever possible. The waiting line for re-entry was getting longer and longer. Tetta knew that those exiting the body now might need to wait millennia to reincarnate if the world didn't drastically change in the very near future. There just wouldn't be enough bodies for souls to get into. Of course, she knew that reincarnation was just for those who believed in it and that those who believed they would see eternal peace would feel content for many centuries of their wait.

103

Tetta could see that all three of the human subjects before her had come into this life on the Karma card and she longed for them to live long enough to exit the karmic dream. Nirvana, she knew, awaited anyone who could truly open himself or herself to it. The hardest part of her work was keeping to herself when her projects continued to clutch their self-limiting ideas. Amelia, Miguel, and Jojo were very open to change. Tetta just wished they knew that they were.

*Pause, pause, pause...*

"Ladies and Gentlemen!" The Ring Master called through a bullhorn. "Little girls and boys!" The audience was filled with the sounds of shushing parents and tittering children. "Welcome to Drury Brother's Circus on Wheels!" The audience erupted in applause. "I would like to draw your attention to the center ring."

A spotlight shone from high above onto the sawdust in the center ring. "And welcome if you will, Dandy the dancing elephant!" Even Amelia felt a jolt of excitement go through her as music came blaring across the big top and a small elephant sashayed into the spotlight wearing a tutu.

Without any human instruction whatsoever Dandy followed the tempo of the music nodding her head. She turned first to her left and then to her right. She held up her right front foot and hopped on her left then alternated her feet differently with every beat.

A man emerged from the shadows and held out his hand. Dandy applied the tip of her trunk to his hand and waltzed with him to and fro, from side to side, then bowed to the audience in all four directions. The crowd applauded happily.

Another elephant entered the ring and put its feet up on a huge red ball. Pushing it aside with his trunk, he placed the top of his head in the sawdust and kicked up his heels until his body rose up and he attained a headstand that lasted very nearly 30 seconds before his feet came back to earth.

"Look!" Jojo pointed into the canopy of the big top. Amelia followed his finger as it dissolved into the air. High above Jojo rematerialized on a platform connected to a pole. He looked down. In his hand was a feather. Beside him on the platform was his trusty snail Dumbo who had grown to the height of Jojo's knee.

"C'mon Jojo!" the snail cheered him on. "You can do it!"

Jojo looked out at the crowd far below. "You want me to jump?" Jojo yelled above the roar of the crowd, sights fixed on him.

"Not jump," Dumbo corrected him, "fly!"

"But last time I flew was on your back!" Jojo yelled.

"It's your turn to fly," the snail insisted. Jojo looked down. The clowns were circling under the towering platform and starting to make fun of him.

"Ohh Nooooo!" one cried and knocked his knees together. The crowd laughed. Another clown ran to the drum an elephant had been standing on just a moment before and cried out, "Heeeelllllp! Oh! Help me I might fall!" The words floated out of his mouth like words in a comic strip. In big balloons they floated up to Jojo and popped around him in midair releasing the jabs and jokes. Jojo became increasingly angry.

"I can't fly!" He looked at the snail.

"Yes you can. Just put your courage in the feather and raise it up."

Jojo tried to do what the snail suggested. "I can't." He hung his head dejectedly.

"Don't *try* Jojo. Do it. You haven't done it *yet,* but you can do it NOW!"

The boy looked at his own two feet on the edge of the platform. He had learned to look at his feet a lot. When adults were angry with him, as was often the case, there seemed to be no safe place to look, and no safe way to look. If he looked an adult in the eye, they wanted to know what he was looking at or would tell him to get that look off his face. Jojo didn't know what he looked like to them. But he knew what his feet looked like. Just one glimpse of his gym shoes made him feel small and small is what most adults seemed to want him to look like.

"You can do it, Jojo!" A new yet familiar voice called up from the stands. He looked down his left arm, past the edge of the platform and saw Amelia waving to him. Something shifted in Jojo's heart and he could sense the faith he had lost in himself. He smiled and the feeling grew. "Go Jojooooo!" Amelia was jumping up and down and cheering.

Jojo looked at the feather and imagined it was magic. *Fill it up with your courage,* Dumbo the snail thought to him. Jojo heard the words as if they were his own thoughts. It seemed as if the feather was growing strong, filling up. It seemed to shine in his hand.

*Hold out your courage and follow it, Jojo,* the snail thought into Jojo's mind. Jojo held out the feather and felt his feet begin to feel lighter. He focused on the feather and pushed off the platform into the air. Then without warning Jojo began to plummet. He felt the air begin to rush past him and heard the noise of the crowd come to an astonished halt. No one made a sound. As he fell Jojo remembered the little mouse that urged Dumbo to pull up and fly. There was no mouse in Jojo's hat. He didn't hear anyone urging him to fly anymore.

*I knew you couldn't do it!* Jojo heard inside his head, but this time he recognized the voice was not his own. He looked down and saw a mean looking clown who started to laugh as Jojo fell closer to the floor. Jojo clenched the feather in his hand and dove toward the clown in a rage.

"You're not funny!" he shouted.

"I don't need to be funny!" the clown shot back. "You're the big joke."

Jojo came within inches of the evil looking clown then pulled up, flying back into the heights of the big top. The crowd cheered. Jojo looked around. He was hovering in midair like a hummingbird.

The clown pulled a sword from a sheath on his side and strode across the floor until he was under Jojo. "Bring your sorry butt down here."

"No problem." Jojo shrugged and dove toward the clown who raised his sword in a menacing gesture. Jojo zipped around behind the clown faster than he could react and putting both hands out knocked the clown to the ground. Jojo landed and his feather grew into an immense sword three times as big as the clown's.

The clown grabbed his sword on the ground and stood to turn. Jojo nonchalantly twirled his big sword with two fingers, seemingly without fear. The clown charged at Jojo who bopped him sideways with his large sword. The clown flew past Jojo and landed in the sawdust near the stands. His sword skittered deeply into the sawdust. Finding it, he raised it up overhead and turned to face Jojo.

"You still here?" Jojo asked.

"Yeah, but you're not going to be for long!"

The clown sliced his sword overhead and cut through a rope. Jojo looked up. A huge bag of sand was falling toward him. He dove to escape and heard the sand land behind him sounding like a door slamming shut. He turned his head to look and bumped it on something. His head dropped to the floor as he saw big shoes walking toward him through the space under his bed.

*Pause, pause, pause...*

"Come on outta' there now, boy." The voice was the same as the clown's.

"Darius!" Jojo whispered too loud.

"Damn right, and I'm done with this trash, now come out from under 'dare or I'm gonna' whoop you." Darius kicked under the bed and Jojo scooted to the other side, his back against the baseboard.

One thing was certain; Darius would whoop him hard if he came out from under the bed. The chances were better for Jojo if he just

107

maintained his position and forced Darius to work for his quarry.

"I didn't do anything," Jojo protested.

"No, you never do anything. That's the problem." Darius kicked under the bed again. "Now where's my box?"

"I don't know!" Jojo felt Darius' foot poking under the other side of the bed and scooted the other way.

"Boy, don't mess with me. I know you got my box, now where is it?!"

"I didn't get it!" Jojo yelled.

"You didn't go where I told you to go?" The vibration of Darius' voice grew louder and more stressed.

"I did!" Jojo insisted.

"Then where is the package?" Darius was down on his hands and feet next to the bed and Jojo felt his time was running out.

"There wasn't one. Nobody was there," he explained knowing it was useless. It didn't matter that he had been where he was told to be. Nor did it matter that he hadn't been given the package Darius was expecting. All that was important right now was that Darius wanted to capture Jojo and Jojo needed to avoid that.

"Pssst!" Jojo heard from under the bed beside him. He looked and saw Dumbo eyeing him through the end of his long tubules. "Get in here." The snail pulled back his belly as if to make an opening for Jojo into the shell.

"I can't fit in there. I'm too big." Jojo considered the dilemma that followed him wherever he went. Either he was too big or too small to get what he needed. He wanted to cry out for his momma but he knew she couldn't hear him. Jojo wished he could be small enough to fit in the snail shell and, as if by magic, he began to shrink smaller and smaller.

"Where'd you go?" He heard Darius' surprised last words as he crawled inside the shell with Dumbo and stayed very quiet.

Jojo felt the shell rock as Darius swung his arm past it through the socks and shoes that were under the bed. Then the room fell silent.

The inside of the snail shell was spacious. Jojo found himself walking on the back of the snail as if it were carpeting. Jojo felt the floor undulating and one tubular eye extended in through the opening of the shell.

"How's everything going on this end?" Dumbo inquired with a distinct British accent. The snail's eye was larger than Jojo's head and the kaleidoscopic details of it were mesmerizing.

"Wow, this is cool!" A pile of pillows appeared and Jojo fell onto them as Dumbo ducked out and the shell started to move. "Where are we going, Dumbo?" The shell jolted to a stop and the snail stuck his eye back inside the pearlescent interior.

"Don't you think it's time we left the Dumbo thing behind?" The snail's entire head moved inside the shell with Jojo, and there was still plenty of room.

"Don't you like being called Dumbo?" Jojo felt a little sadness come over him.

"Listen kid, I'm not a little elephant. I'm a snail. And a pretty magical one at that, if you don't mind me saying so," the snail replied. "I'm no Dumbo and neither are you." Jojo's chin dropped to his chest. "Now, stop that," the snail continued. "Pouting won't get you anywhere and you didn't do anything wrong." The snail nudged the boy with what might have been his nose, if snails did indeed possess noses. "Wouldn't you like to know my real name?"

Jojo's attitude brightened. "You had a name before I named you Dumbo?"

"Why sure I did." If snails could smile, this one did.

"What is it?" Jojo was excited.

The snail thought for a moment. "Okay, so I lied just then. Snails don't have names," the snail admitted. "But I'd like to have one that showed off my true potential. You and me buddy, we're in this together now. How 'bout you help me come up with a proper name?"

Jojo thought about his own name. He had a proper name Joseph

John Jenkins and his nickname Jojo. Sometimes when his teacher was mad at him she called him Joseph John. That's when he knew she meant business. Other times, when they were having fun in class, she would call him Jojo and he felt like she liked him a lot. One time she had read a poem out of a small thin book about cats. In the poem it said that every cat had at least three different names. Jojo looked at the snail trying to ascertain what the rules for naming a snail might be. Dumbo was special. Jojo liked the name Dumbo.

The snail could see this was going to take awhile and he anticipated he might not like the new name Jojo might give him anymore than the old name. "I heard this one once," the snail volunteered. "It's from a poem about a knight who went on a quest a long, long time ago."

"Quest?" Jojo asked

"A trip, a journey," the snail clarified.

"Are we on a quest?"

"We will be as soon as I get my head out of this hole," the snail nodded.

"What was the name?" Jojo asked.

"Sir Galahad." The snail smiled, as much as snails do, at the way the words sounded when he said them.

"Sir Galahad," Jojo repeated. "Was he a good guy?"

"Really good."

"Too good to have fun?"

"No, good enough to have a lot of big adventures." *After he got out of the nunnery,* the snail thought.

"Okay," Jojo agreed to the name change.

"Great." The snail started to pull his head back out of the shell.

"Sir Gala...Sir Gala..." Jojo tried to call the snail.

"Galahad," the snail filled in, rolling his tubular eye back toward Jojo.

"Are we going to have an adventure now?" Jojo asked.

"When was the last time you traveled via the inside of a snail's shell?" the snail replied.

"Sir Gala…"

"Galahad!" The snail sighed.

"I think you need a nickname. This one is too long."
The snail frowned at the boy. He liked his name. "What would you suggest?"

Jojo smiled then shouted with enthusiasm, "DUMBO!"

"Why don't you take a nap?" The snail slunk his head out of the shell and the rig began to move not unlike the howdah on top of Hrim's back in the jungle.

*Pause, pause, pause…*

Amelia stood staring at the phone in the living room of the cottage on Main Street. It was nighttime and the room was dark. She looked down. The gold lamé shoes were missing which she now recognized as a sign that she was dreaming within her dream. She was wearing the flannel pajamas she had worn since she arrived in small town America. It seemed she had awakened in her dream when the phone started ringing. As it continued to ring she saw again the last scene she could remember from the circus. Jojo had fallen from the platform on the tower and disappeared into thin air. Amelia tried to calm down by reminding herself that it was only a dream. Nevertheless, her concern continued to grow as Jojo failed to rematerialize.

As Amelia listened to the phone ring she wondered if it could be some news about Jojo. Picking up the receiver she answered. "Hello?"

"We have a very important message for Amelia Bradford," the voice on the other end of the line began.

*Telemarketer,* Amelia started to dismiss the call, and began hanging up.

"We have been trying to reach you and it is urgent that we speak to you right away." Amelia brought the receiver back to her ear tightly. "Please call us at 888-341-SHOE. Your ID number is 5001. Please refer to this number when you call. Our hours are running out. Again, we have an urgent message for you. Please call us right away. Ask for Miss Northrup." The message completed and the call disconnected. Amelia frantically tried to remember the number.

*888. No, never mind that, you'll remember toll-free. 341-SHOE!*

Amelia depressed the buttons to disconnect the call and barely waited to hear the dial tone before she started dialing. She depressed the buttons again and listened closer this time. There was no dial tone.

"Hello?" she whispered into the phone. There was no answer. "Hello?" She felt a sense of urgency rising in her.

"If you'd like to make a call," a pre-recorded phone-company voice stated, "please hang up and try again." Amelia depressed the buttons again and again but no dial tone came through. Finally she shoved the receiver onto the cradle and stared at the phone.

*If the dreamtime works according to my beliefs, then why I can't make a simple phone call?* Amelia noticed the negative affirmation in her thoughts. She turned away from the phone and looked out the window toward the street. Fireflies illuminated the bushes around the houses, while gaslights entertained moths. She felt herself longing for something. It was her own dream, her own life.

*Pause, pause, pause...*

# 6

## Am I Dreaming?

The nineteenth floor of the Regency overlooked the grounds of Withrow High School providing a park-like view not so dissimilar to Central Park in New York.  Sunlight streaming through the solarium windows illuminated the living room walls, which bounced light into the bedroom.  Amelia stirred in her sleep rolling over to the song of her exotic bird from India, a Green Avadat.

"Good morning sweetie."  Amelia smiled in the sunshine taking a deep breath and rolled over onto her back.  *What was I dreaming?* she wondered as Zeke crawled out from under the covers and began licking her face.

"Okay, okay.  Breakfast is coming."  Amelia swung her legs over the edge of the bed and let their weight carry her body to a sitting position.  She looked at the clock.  Five?  I'm up ahead of the alarm.  She imagined her early rising must have something to do with her excitement about the trip.  Amelia pulled on her chenille robe and

113

tied it around her waist then lifted Zeke onto the floor. She padded across the hardwood floor and slipped her feet into her favorite fuzzy blue slippers. A scene from the Wizard of Oz was playing in her mind.

"I had a dream last night," she said aloud. "And you and you and," she looked around the room ending with Zeke, "and you were in it!" she said dramatically.

Zeke yelped.

"Oh, you remember being there?" She smiled as she padded into the kitchen and poured a cup of food into Zeke's bowl. "There were a lot of characters there, though I can't quite remember them." *Oh, I shouldn't say that,* Amelia thought. "I'll remember in time," she corrected.

Amelia pushed the button on her state of the art coffee maker that sequentially ground the coffee beans, added water, and brewed. The grinding process sounded like a jet engine was about to take off in the kitchen.

Amelia opened the cabinet door over the coffee maker and began opening bottles of supplements dumping them out in one, two, and three pill combinations. She opened the refrigerator and pulled a loaf of low-carb, whole grain bread from the top shelf. Untwisting the plastic covered wire seal, she pulled one piece of bread out of the bag and lowered it into the toaster.

As part of her regular morning routine she went to the door and opened it to reveal the New York Times sitting on the welcome mat. Stooping to pick it up she glanced at the powder blue fuzzy slippers and couldn't help but feel as if something was strangely different.

Amelia laid the paper on the table in the solarium, circled back toward the kitchen, cruised by the toaster and landed the piece of crusty bread on her plate. Deftly, her hand moved to the coffee urn pouring it into the cup which had come out of the cabinet along with her vitamins. Reaching inside the refrigerator she grabbed a jar of marmalade and let the door fall closed as she completed her journey to a wicker chair in the solarium while balancing her breakfast collection in both hands.

Sipping from her cup, she looked out over the treetops that stretched on for blocks. There was so much to do before the flight left that evening, but it was important to Amelia that she didn't short herself on the time she needed to start her day off right.

Amelia was determined to make this a good trip. Though the circumstances surrounding her journey had changed, she felt she had salvaged the best possible outcome from the entire situation.

For a moment she dared to think about David and the two years that had ended up in the toilet two weeks ago. Amelia wasn't inclined to be an emotional wreck after she ended their engagement. In a way, it was like a business plan gone bad, and Amelia was ruthless in business.

The phone rang and Amelia reached to answer it. Without a thought apparently linked to the motion, her hand suddenly pulled back as if it didn't want to answer the phone. *Odd*, Amelia thought, and picked up the receiver.

"Hello, Mother," she guessed.

"How did you know it was me? I didn't star-82," Amelia's mom replied.

"It's 5:32 a.m., Mom. Who else would be calling me?"

"True. True." Karen Bradford gathered her paper list into her hands preparing to read into the phone. "Honey, I have a checklist here and I thought things might go better if we synchronized our day."

"Right now I'm drinking my morning coffee. And you?"

"All right, Smartie. What about last minute shopping? Do you need anything?"

"I'm sure I will and I'll make a list after I finish my toast." Amelia hugged the phone to her head with her shoulder while she scooped orange marmalade out of a jar with a knife. "Mom, can I call you back? I'm really very excited, but I just need a few minutes before I barrel ahead." The silence that was Karen Bradford thinking her daughter was making a mistake was loud and clear. She took a deep breath and did her best to intonate something other than the 'I don't care, do what you want' message that was most likely to fill her reply.

"Okay, give me a call after you're showered and ready to go."

"Mom, don't wait." Amelia whined by reflex.

"I won't. I have a cell phone now, call me and let me know what you need."

"Okay." Amelia rolled her eyes. She was happy her mom could come on the trip but wasn't sure how their very different ways of handling agendas was going to interplay.

"Love you, bye," her mom concluded the conversation.

"Okay, bye," Amelia replied.

Amelia's mother had started concluding phone calls with the atypical "Love you, bye" after Amelia's father passed away. Amelia imagined it was her mother's attempt to make sure she never regretted not saying it, though she couldn't imagine her mother feared either of them was going to die anytime soon. Amelia found it easy to believe that her mother and father rarely exchanged an expression of love. James Bradford had been a calculating businessman in the office and at home. Amelia was very much like him, though he specialized in accounting and she in law.

Karen Bradford on the other hand was a bleeding heart schoolteacher who took every tough case home with her. In addition to professing her love at the end of phone calls after her dad died, Amelia's mom had started sharing her tough cases with Amelia. It was one of the few things the mother and daughter had in common. Though a corporate lawyer, Amelia did her share of pro bono work for the needy.

Amelia's mind wandered to the latest case her mom had brought to her attention. There were just a few phone calls she should make to assure that details were handled properly in her absence.

Reaching in her purse she pushed the button on her PDA and searched for the home number of the associate lawyer who was on the case.

Trisha Jennings had been with the firm for three years and longed to move up the ladder. Amelia wanted to see Trisha through a little well-rounded experience before moving her into a supervisory position. At 36, Amelia loved to bring young lawyers to the firm. There was, however, always an element of competition between the like-aged co-workers over which she needed to constantly assert herself. Trisha often too easily juxtaposed herself as an equal to Amelia.

Amelia was personally supervising the often-adversarial Trisha as a way to keep her enemy closer. Trisha was promising to be as ruthless as Amelia in the corporate law setting. Amelia also wanted to see that Trisha was capable of being equally compassionate in the personal setting.

By making Trisha Guardian ad Litem to Joseph John Jenkins she hoped to give Trisha the space to practice compassion and understanding. The boy had been removed enough times to end up in permanent custody and this latest event might well require such measures since his stepfather had been charged with physical abuse a few days earlier.

Amelia contemplated the delicate issues surrounding the case and decided that it might be better if she met with the boy personally to talk with him as his teacher's daughter rather than let Trisha have first crack at him in her typical corporate lawyer tone.

Getting up from the table Amelia headed for the shower. She decided she would call Trisha later to let her know of her plans. If she was going to squeeze in a personal visit before she left, she might just need to phone in her last minute shopping order to her mother after all.

*Pause, pause, pause...*

Karen Bradford drove toward the mall with her headset securely clipped to her collar. She didn't like driving with the ear bud in place. She felt it looked like she was wearing a hearing aid. At sixty, Karen was becoming increasingly conscientious about her appearance. As she noticed crow's feet gathering around her daughters' eyes she couldn't deny her own crows feet were growing deeper and deeper.

By focusing more on her thickening jowls and fuzzy cheeks she had become less likely to notice and draw out the younger looking qualities elsewhere in her physique. While she was a powerful teacher to others, Karen often failed to demonstrate exactly what she encouraged others to overcome. She would scold her students, and even strangers in the grocery line for their negative attitudes, while acting on her own.

Knowing this about herself was what played through Karen's mind as she became increasingly fearful that her daughter would grow impatient with her habits over the two weeks they would be in India.

*She'll probably leave me somewhere and I'll need to be rescued by some monk,* Karen thought. *But maybe I'll learn something important from some sort of a guru while I'm there and that will change everything.* As her inner voice whined on inside her head she snapped her fingers in front of her face over the steering wheel.

"Snap out of it!" she ordered herself.

Karen's habit of belittling herself was a behavior Amelia refused to tolerate. She would never forget the argument they had right after Amelia's dad died. It ended with Amelia pointing in Karen's face and delivering the warning, "I'm not here to convince you that you're good enough. And I'm not going to waste my life waiting for you to approve of me." With that argument, Amelia had stopped validating Karen as compensation for her insecurities.

Karen knew she had shifted her dependence for external validation from her husband to her daughter. However, she had failed to consider that her daughter, with her life so seemingly altogether, continued to have inner doubts about herself and her relationship with her parents. For a long time Karen had tried to blame her daughter's emotional evasiveness on the death of her father. Over time, however, she had accepted it was a wall both she and her husband had helped build long before he died. Through the years Karen had done a lot of study and work to undo her way of gaining negative attention by comparing and belittling herself. Today she needed everything she knew to kick in all at once.

The cell phone vibrated and bleeped its ring tone next to Karen on the car seat. She loaded the ear bud and pressed the button that answered the call.

"Hello?" Karen yelled through the headset as though she were calling across a valley to hear an echo bounce back.

"Hi Mom." Amelia held the phone away from her ear.

"Hey, how's everything going?"

"Just fine," Amelia replied, anticipating her mother's dissatisfaction as she delivered her update. "I just finished my shower and thought I'd check in on your little boy before we leave. Do you have the number for his foster parent?"

Karen glanced at the digital clock in the car. She was amazed that her daughter was just exiting the shower at 7:30. *The clock is 5 minutes fast,* Karen negotiated with her inner critic, *but the day is practically half over.* Karen feared the critic might win. Opting to express gratitude that Amelia was going to pay a personal visit to her student, Karen shifted from judgmental back to helpful.

"Okay, are you ready?"

"You have the number for the foster parent memorized?" Amelia was surprised.

"No," Karen laughed, "you can reach him through district two. Detective Alvarez. He's helped several of my kids. He provides temporary housing for some kids and he's fostering Jojo."

Amelia couldn't imagine why her mother never moved to a neighborhood school that had fewer incidents of drugs and abuse among the families.

"Call him at the station," Karen directed.

"Okay, I'll do that."

"So," Karen ventured, "do you need me to get anything?" Karen caught her obsessive helpfulness going into action and held back making suggestions of personal items she thought Amelia might need.

"Probably will since I'm seeing Joseph, but I'll need to get back to you on that." Karen caught herself wanting to go to the ultimatum level and telling Amelia she was in the parking lot of the Super Saver right now and she needed her to think fast.

"Okay," Karen held back, "if I'm still out and about I'll be happy to get something for you." Amelia could detect the guilt trip forming on the horizon.

"I'll call you as I go, Mom. I promise."

"Okay, love you, bye." Karen depressed the button on the cord of her headset and felt successful in not crossing Amelia's big boundaries.

Amelia put down the receiver reminding herself that she needed to make some room for her mother in her life for the next two weeks if either of them were going to have a good time.

As Amelia blew her hair dry she again noticed the fuzzy slippers now lying on the bathroom floor. *Oh shit!* she thought, *I never got the hiking shoes.* Amelia remembered the argument she had with David two weeks earlier in his shoe store.

So much had changed since they had first met in his shoe store. David had established his store to be cutting edge. He had poured his entire savings into stocking it with shoes from the best, priciest, European designers. Three months later he was struggling to keep it afloat. Amelia liked his mannerisms and the selection of shoes and

120

took David on like a pro-bono client, supporting him by throwing parties in his store and wrangling patronage out of her friends and associates. Over the next few months, Amelia didn't stop to question as the relationship shifted to become more personal than professional.

It was almost eighteen months later as they were about to be married that Amelia was able to see that the longer they were together, the more David's attention for both her and the store seemed to be waning.

When Amelia stopped in unexpectedly to search for shoes for both the wedding and their honeymoon, David had appeared unusually nervous and upset. It was as if he didn't have time for her. He kept trying to rush her out of the store with shoes she didn't want.

"Take these," he said, "I'll see you at seven." David had literally shoved the open box of gold lamé shoes into her hands. When Amelia became equally obsessed with not taking the shoes she forgot all about the hiking shoes and left the store empty handed. There wasn't another store in town that would carry the shoes she wanted.

Checking her watch she knew that David wouldn't be in the store until after noon. Brushing her teeth Amelia decided to stop there first and get the shoes early so she didn't have to deal with David. Grabbing her purse she remembered to call information to get the number for District 2. Plugging the number into her cell phone Amelia proceeded to leave the condominium complex as she did everyday, completely unaware of her surroundings.

Without a thought she pushed the buttons for the elevator that delivered her to the lobby. She didn't make eye contact with or acknowledge the concierge in any way. She held out her keys for the valet. As he ran to get her car, Amelia waited on hold to speak with Detective Alvarez.

"This is Detective Alvarez." The voice sounded strangely familiar to Amelia, but she dismissed the connection as impossible since she did no criminal work.

"Hello Detective. This is Amelia Bradford of Bradford &

Associates Law Firm. We are handling the case for Joseph John Jenkins. I was hoping I might be able to visit Joseph this morning before I leave on a trip."

Miguel Alvarez took a deep breath to keep from losing his temper with the lawyer. *Thanks for the advance notice,* he thought.

"Sure." Detective Alvarez tried to sound friendly, "He's at home with the sitter. Five Thousand One Northrup," he volunteered.

Amelia slid into her car as she flipped open her PDA and wrote a note with her stylus on the screen. "Five-Zero-Zero-One Northrup," she double checked. "Where is that?" she asked, not recognizing the street name.

"South Avondale." Detective Alvarez was fairly certain she had never been in the neighborhood. He offered instructions. "From Victory Parkway head west on King. Turn left on Vernon. It's 6 blocks down on the left. Park on the street. Lock your door. Don't pay any attention to the guys in the white t-shirts. If they think they can bother you, they will."

Amelia's brow furrowed as she tried to determine why a police officer would live in such a bad part of town. Detective Alvarez understood the importance of foster kids being located in neighborhoods close to their cousins and places they knew.

"So I can stop by any time?" Amelia asked, not even considering her last minute call or visit could seem invasive.

"Of course." Detective Alvarez realized the futility of trying to obtain respect from a high power attorney doing her good deed for the year.

"I will be in India for two weeks," Amelia advised him. "If there's anything you need, you may contact my associate, Trisha Jennings at 555-8100."

"Thanks." Detective Alvarez wrote the name and number on the pad in front of him. *India,* he thought. *Must be nice.*

"The sitter's name is Alicia," the detective advised in return. "I'll give her a call to let her know you are on your way so she can make sure Jojo is around to meet you. Do you know when you might stop by?" The detective decided he could try to pin her down.

Amelia thought of the boy being kept inside on a sunny day. "Probably not until 3:00 this afternoon," she answered. "If there's some problem just call the service, 555-4667. They'll track me down." Her phone bleeped with an incoming call from her mother.

"Detective, I have a call I must take. Good-bye." Amelia didn't wait to hear his response. She swapped the call to pick up the call from her mother.

"Where are you now?" her mom asked. The business of getting out of town was in full swing.

"I'm on 4$^{th}$ Street," Amelia replied.

"Doing what?" Karen Bradford missed an opportunity to respect her daughter's boundaries. "Oh for God's sake, Amelia. You're not stopping by David's store!"

"Mom," Amelia sighed, "I need hiking shoes."

"Can't you get them somewhere else? Why do you want to bring this up today?"

"Mom, I'm not going to see David, and for your information *this* is already up today!" She felt the heat rising in her cheeks and wondered how it was that she could control her temper in court but not in the presence of her mother.

"Okay. I'm sorry." Amelia's mom backed off first before she dug herself too deep of a hole.

"I'm sorry too, Mom." Amelia was able to respond to her mom's reversal. "I really don't think I'm trying to start anything. I just want the shoes and David won't be there if I go now."

"Okay, no need to explain," Karen finished it. "I'm at the pharmacy, is there anything you need? Mini shampoo? Toothpaste?" Once Karen Bradford crossed boundaries, she had a hard time locating them again.

*Pause, pause, pause...*

Miguel Alvarez turned from his computer and stared out the window of his office, across the parking lot of District 2 Headquarters to the tea lined windows of the Coffee Emporium across the street. He felt he was in a race against time. With what, he didn't know. Seldom did he feel such a compelling need to solve a drug running case.

The District 2 jurisdiction ran from Madisonville to Hyde Park. He worked with cases involving the poorest to the richest. Before he made detective, Miguel ran a street beat in Madisonville. At night he would often drive up to the busiest corners and scare off big expensive cars. Often when he ran the plates he found that the cars belonged to residents from richer neighborhoods.

Despite the differences one might anticipate between the rich and poor, Miguel had found the problems were often the same. The difference was that rich people could hire powerful attorneys to get them out of trouble while the poor couldn't afford to manipulate the law. What bothered him most was when he saw the future of many of the kids who got caught in the middle. Joseph was one of those cases and Miguel was determined to see that he didn't slip through the cracks.

Alvarez thought about the lady lawyer showing up at the last minute before she took off on vacation. He was glad he would be home by one and meet her at three. That way he could make sure she understood the importance of the case. He checked his watch. There were four hours left in his shift. *Maybe I can get some of these pieces to fall together,* he thought.

Miguel Alvarez opened the file that was thick with Post-It notes of every color. Grabbing onto the closest goldenrod colored note he separated the pages and looked at the mug shot of Darius Lovelle. There was nothing loving about the appearances of the man who was Jojo's stepfather. Dark circles dug in deep under huge brown eyes tinted with red broken blood vessels and overhung by heavy lids. Lovelle's general expression was contemptuous and without care.

When Miguel interviewed Joseph he indicated his step-father was angry with him because he failed to pick-up a package Lovelle had sent him to retrieve. The boy didn't know what was in the package. He had been told to wait for it in the alley behind a shoe store on 4th street, but swore that no one ever showed up to give him anything so he went home.

Miguel went with the caseworker to retrieve Joseph's things from the apartment where he lived with his stepfather. The boy came out of his bedroom carrying a clear rectangular box in one hand while dragging his clothing in a pillowcase with the other.

"What do you have in there?" Miguel had crouched on the floor in front of the boy to look inside the container. "It's Dumbo, my teacher's snail." Joseph didn't offer the detective a closer look.

"Don't you have anything else you would like to bring along?" Detective Alvarez asked. The boy hung his head low.

"No, just this." The boy held the clear box closer to his chest. "I'll be home soon," Joseph replied.

Miguel was amazed at children's desires to stay in the home even if it was an uncomfortable or dangerous place. He figured it had something to do with the need to feel loved by their parents or, perhaps, a reluctance to give up their role as caretaker for their parents. Joseph's teacher had referred his case to the Department of Human Services and Detective Alvarez. After he met with Joseph at school he explained to the teacher how the boy tried to convince him that the bruises had been sustained in a bike crash.

"Let's face it, officer," Karen Bradford explained it the way she saw it, "what are his prospects in foster care? How can he trust anyone in an official capacity when the closest thing he has to family has let him down?" It made sense to Miguel Alvarez. Having been raised in a loving, supportive environment, Detective Alvarez felt he had something to offer and was glad to take Joseph in for a while.

Miguel searched through his notes on the facing page and copied the name of the shoe store where Jojo said he had waited. Looking up the address online, he decided to stop by the shop and ask if they had noticed any unwanted presence on the street or behind the shop. Maybe they could identify Darius or provide additional information. Alvarez was determined to shut down not just the end points but also the entire ring that would use kids to run illegal drugs and money, or whatever was in the box that idiots believed was important enough to hit a child.

*Pause, pause, pause...*

Amelia rounded the corner of 4th and Vine for the third time, which ended up being the charm, providing her a parking spot right in front of the door of Des Shoes, David's European Shoe Store. Praying she had been right that David would not be at the store at 10:00 in the morning she entered and walked directly to the hiking boots she wanted. She scanned the shelves for the Weathermax full-grain leather shoes with waxed stitching. Remembering the informational insert she found in the shoebox on her previous visit, she knew the hiking shoe sported a vegetable-tanned, metal-free leather insole made with perforated felt to ensure good air circulation.

"Amelia?" The clerk smiled.

"Hello Shima." Amelia smiled back into the dark eyes. Amelia's relationship with Shima had always been slightly strained but today it felt as though chasms and valleys extended for miles between them. Amelia could see that Shima detected her animosity. She never had learned how to hide it with Shima. *Then again,* Amelia thought, *how am I supposed to feel? It's been three weeks since I broke up with David and I haven't heard one word of consolation from her.*

"Is there something I can do?" Shima asked.

*Too little, too late,* Amelia thought. Amelia found the hiking shoes on the shelf and picked them up.

"Do you have these in a size 7?"

"I would have to check." Shima practically sneered in recognition of Amelia's desire to put her in her place. The clerk disappeared into the back of the store and Amelia regretted being so short with her.

While she waited, Amelia's eyes drifted over to the gold lamé shoes she and David had argued about. She moved toward them slowly. How could he have wanted her to take those? The open toe sandal featured a heel sling with a metal buckle and sparkling vines twining atop the straps. The tapered high heel would have lifted Amelia way off center. *How does one balance on something like that?* Amelia wondered. She looked down at her own practical loafers. Obviously she had gotten her shoe gene from her mother.

Picking up one of the sandals Amelia was suddenly flooded with a strange feeling of déjà vu. At once she felt lost and found, fearful and angry, hot and cold, dizzy and suffocated. She dropped the shoe on the floor and staggered back a step.

"I'll get it." Amelia looked down to see Shima reaching for the shoe on the floor. Shima recognized the shoe over which David and Amelia had fought in the store. She quietly placed the shoe back on its stand and extended the box of hiking boots toward Amelia. "These are more your style." Shima acknowledged what she knew of Amelia's taste in personal attire.

For a moment Amelia felt as if her eyes might fill with tears. She quickly focused her attention inside her handbag and produced her American Express card. "Please take care of it," she asked, without trying on the hiking shoes. *If they don't fit, they won't go to India.* All she wanted at that moment was to escape the store and Shima.

Shima completed the transaction quickly and bagged the box for Amelia. Putting her hand on Amelia's elbow, Shima walked her toward the door. "Send me a postcard from my home town." Shima looked to see if Amelia acknowledged her comment. There was no eye contact. Amelia had never really explored Shima's connection with India and she didn't feel any interest now.

GOLD LAMÉ

"I will." Amelia couldn't muster any more friendliness. She smiled weakly, quickly walked through the door, and popped the locks on her Mercedes SUV.

*Pause, pause, pause...*

As the doorknob pulled away from her hand and closed behind Amelia, Shima dazed into memories of her life on the train platforms of India. She had been living on the streets as an orphan for about 3 months after her mother disappeared, when she was abducted by two local men and taken to a room in the local hotel used by tourists.

Shima had heard stories about what would happen next. She had accepted it as her destiny. When the nuns from the local monastery had tried to save her from the inevitable future she faced, Shima fiercely resisted them. At age ten she believed she had done something to cause her mother to disappear. She didn't want help from anyone. She was on her own.

When the man entered the room Shima felt her heart skip a beat. He looked so different from the local men who teased and cajoled her on the train platform. Her visitor was tall and looked elegant with smooth black hair, a dark gray suit, and neatly trimmed moustache. He towered over her and looked deeply into her eyes. As he did, she saw his eyes were wet with tears. Uncomfortable with this show of emotion, Shima had moved away, but he didn't pursue her or ask her to do anything. Instead, he began by asking her age.

"Fourteen." she lied, using the perfect English her mother had taught her.

"Really?" He seemed surprised and gave her a stern look.

"Ten." She revised her answer, feeling much the same as when she disappointed a teacher in school.

"I thought so." He nodded and paced a couple steps thoughtfully.

"Are you from the government?" Shima became wary of the purpose of the visit.

"No," he replied. "I am from America." Shima again resigned herself to the possibility of no good coming from this encounter. "I worked with the government awhile ago and that is why I have returned. I was looking for someone, but was unable to locate her. You remind me of her."

"So?" she asked. "Who was she?"

"Just a friend." The man answered and walked farther across the room to look out the window. "You are homeless?" he asked without turning around. Shima felt especially lonely standing in the middle of the large suite at that moment.

"No, I live with my friends," Shima sputtered.

"At the train station." Shima winced at the judgmental tone in his voice.

"Yes." She jutted out her chin in an effort to look proud.

"Well little girl," the man began, "I miss my friend very much and I was wondering if you might like to come home with me to America in her place?"

Shima was not prepared for this. She thought she might have to endure the man for a day, maybe a night, and then she could return to the station. The idea that he would take her away from all she knew was frightening to her. She thought of running from the room while the man had his back turned. But she knew her abductors could not be far away.

"I wish to adopt you as my daughter," the man continued. "I will give you a good home and fine education in the land of opportunity." He turned around and saw that she was alarmed. He crossed the floor and reached for her hand. She pulled away and he crouched down to her eye level.

"I have a daughter just a little younger than you. Her name is Amelia and she would love a new sister." He tried to reassure Shima. She looked at him carefully. She surmised that this was a one-time offer and the next man would not be as kind.

The man reached for her hand again, and she allowed him to hold it. She waited for some sign of the abuse she had been experiencing around the train station, but there was none of it. At the same time she knew this wasn't a decision she could make. If she had been abducted, then she was already bought and paid for. All she could do was hope for the best then, and she nodded that she would go with him.

As it turned out, Amelia had had not been thrilled that Shima had come home to be her sister. Shima never felt secure with the Bradfords. She spent her days simultaneously trying to fit in while resisting any inclination to care. Even after Jim Bradford's death, she yearned for a sense of belonging in the place she would not call home.

*Pause, pause, pause...*

Detective Miguel Alvarez pulled past the Mercedes SUV and parked in front of it in a space reserved for taxis outside the shoe store. Amelia pulled away and glanced at the city police tags on the car.

*Nice to be able to break the law when you're the enforcer,* she thought.

Miguel waited until the Mercedes cleared the side of his car and manually locked the doors as he exited his plain white Hyundai. When he walked through the entrance of Des Shoe, his dark eyes met with Shima's. Miguel immediately detected distrust.

"Hello, I'm looking for the manager." He was anxious to avoid posturing with the clerk and get down to business.

"I am the manager," Shima tilted back her head and lowered her eyelids dismissingly as she glanced over the detective's worn shirt and jacket.

"Of course. I am Detective Alvarez," Miguel started again while showing his badge. "I am looking into allegations that there is drug running going on around this store. Have you seen anyone suspicious while you've been here?"

Shima bristled. Her days on the train platform had burned an unfading sense of distrust for authority figures in her attitude.

"Detective," Shima glared at Miguel, "this store is posh. We are not in the business of monitoring what goes on in the alley."

"So you have seen trafficking?"

"I didn't say that. I would call the police if I saw anything suspicious. I have to think about the safety of the customers. It's difficult to sell $300 shoes when people are afraid to come to your store."

"I see," said Miguel, looking around the store trying to determine which pair of shoes could possibly cost $300. "Is there anyone else I could talk to while I'm here?"

"There is the owner, but he will not be in for another two hours," Shima put him off.

"Well then, I guess I'll stop back later." Miguel extended his card. "Will you see that he gets this and ask him to call me on Monday?"

"I suppose I can." Shima looked at the card but didn't take it, waiting for Miguel to place it on the countertop. "Good day, Detective." Shima's eyes moved deliberately from his eyes to the door as she impatiently raised her eyebrow.

"Thanks." Miguel nodded, then thought, *Thanks for nothing,* as he left the store. Heading for his car, Miguel checked his watch. He could grab a bite to eat downtown before heading home. *It's not a good idea to meet with a lady lawyer on an empty stomach,* Miguel told himself.

Shima watched as the detective pulled away from the taxi stand. She lifted the store's portable phone to her ear. Shima pressed one button for a moment and speed dial completed the call. After a moment Shima began to speak slowly and deliberately with only the slightest hint of urgency in her voice.

"A detective from the police department just left. He was

inquiring about what I know about drug activity in the area." Shima waited. "Yes, that's him." She waited again. "He's not in yet." Waiting. "Twelve, I would imagine." Listening. "Thanks."

Shima hung up the phone and looked at it for a moment. She grabbed the detective's business card from the counter, then crumpled it in her hand depositing it in the garbage can under the cash register.

*Pause, pause, pause...*

Trisha Jennings' cell phone chirped in the handbag sitting on the chair next to her. She grabbed the phone and checked the number. Rolling her eyes she flipped the phone open and took the call.

"Trisha Jennings." She answered the phone in a flat, informative tone.

"Hi Trisha. It's Amelia." Trisha plunged her fork into the leafy salad on the plate before her.

"Hi Amelia. I thought you would be getting ready to leave." Veiled attempts to sound sweet were unsuccessful.

"I am," Amelia replied. "I just wanted you to know that I talked with a..." Amelia paused as she checked the notes scrawled on the notepad of her palm while continuing to drive, "a Detective Alvarez this morning and I am going to meet with the little boy, Joseph, this afternoon."

Trisha was instantly infused with anger. Amelia was forevermore handing her a case and then taking it back, oftentimes after she had done a significant amount of work. Then Amelia took the credit for the work. It wasn't like Amelia was getting something Trisha should get. After all, Amelia was the owner of the firm. But that was largely because of her wealthy father. Trisha thought the clients should know who was really doing the job that was keeping them happy.

Typically Trisha would view pro bono clients as grunt work that she was well beyond. But hearing that Amelia was butting in on the child abuse case was icing on a two-tiered cake of unwanted interference.

"I met with the boy two days ago, Amelia. Has something new developed?" Trisha sounded defensive.

"Don't take it personally, Trisha." Amelia barely attempted to soothe Trisha's always-too-easy-to-read contempt. "I just had to see him or my mom will be worried the whole time we're in India." Trisha wasn't consoled even though the thought of Amelia spending her botched honeymoon with her mother instead of David Delaney brought a slight smile to Trisha's lips.

"If you would like to come along that would be okay with me," Amelia offered.

"I can't Amelia. It's Friday. I'll be in the Pennington hearing all day." Trisha had been in too many situations where Amelia showed up long enough to undermine her authority on a case only to leave her hanging without support.

"Oh." The trial date had not shown up on Amelia's calendar. "Well, I'll call you afterward to let you know what I think."

*I'm sure you will,* Trisha thought. "Just leave me a message and I'll listen to it when I get a chance," Trisha exerted the little control she could find. Both women ended the call simultaneously without a single departing word.

Trisha second-guessed herself for only a brief moment before deciding everything would be in order and there was no need to change her plans. Everything was being handled professionally and there was no way Amelia could cause any real problems. Turning to her salad, Trisha picked up her knife and began cutting at the leafy lettuce. So she had lied about the Pennington case. That would be long forgotten by the time Amelia returned from India.

*Pause, pause, pause....*

133

As if she hadn't seen it coming all along, Amelia suddenly felt her time was running out. Glancing at her watch she realized she had only two hours to collect Zeke and get him to the kennel, take Binga to Martin's pet store for extra special care while she was gone, pick up her dry cleaning, and get all of the last minute shopping finished. Packing was another venture that needed to be squeezed in. She snapped open her cell phone and dialed the number of fate.

"Hi Mom." Amelia took a deep breath as she silently reminded herself to be patient with her mom.

"Finally ready for a little help?" Karen Bradford didn't mind sounding a little triumphant at this point. She had been counting backward from take-off, figuring their way through homeland security lines, long-term parking, and traffic to determine that they needed to leave for the airport by 4:00. The silence on Amelia's end of the line sunk in and caused Karen to reconsider her tone.

"I mean you only have a couple hours if you're going to see Jojo," Karen tried to backtrack. The name Jojo stuck with Amelia for a moment and then cleared through her temporary irritation as the alternative name for Joseph John.

"Right you are mom. So can you still help me?" Amelia knew she needed the help, "I am thinking on the fly so it is in no way a complete list."

*Of course it's not.* Karen filled in her own silence with candid thoughts that threatened to set them back. *How does she run a business with this level of organizational skill?"*

"Okay," Amelia responded to the silence. "Perhaps I should stop and make a list then call you back."

"No, no. Really," Karen insisted. "I have the cell phone. You can call me as you go and I'll just head for that aisle." Amelia overlooked her tendency to fill in the sarcasm for her mom.

"Okay then." She jumped into the clenches of Karen's two-fisted helpfulness.

"Wait! I can't drive and write!" Karen pulled over to the curb and picked up the shopping list and pen that were waiting for Amelia's additions. "Go!" Karen blurted as if starting a race.

"Okay." Amelia waited for another delay. None was forthcoming. She unwillingly acknowledged a purchase her mother had suggested hours before, "I *do* need a tiny toothpaste, some sort of container for my supplements, lens cleaner, and gum."

Karen looked at the list that seemed to issue forth from her daughter's mind in no particular order. "Feminine protection?" she asked.

"Lucky for you, not on this trip." Amelia gave a laugh that broke the tension. "If it seems I have PMS, you can rest assured it's really your menopause!" They both laughed.

"You'd never survive in this life as a man with that kind of candor!" Karen retorted.

"Oh, I'm sorry." Amelia continued to tease remembering her dad's favorite way to diffuse her mother's temper, "You're right. How is it that you're always right?"

"Now you're talking!" Karen spouted and laughed until a tear came to her eye. Amelia took a deep cleansing breath and quieted her tone.

"Listen, Mom, I'm really glad you're coming with me. I'm sure we're going to have a good time."

"Me too." Karen smiled. She playfully shifted her tone to one of being on a stealth mission, "I'm going in." She put down the pen and paper and turned back onto the road. "Call me if you have any further instructions!"

"Check and double check!" Amelia adapted another of her father's favorite clearings for executing the vacation checklist.

Ten minutes after Karen Bradford entered Trifles discount store the cell phone vibrated on her hip. Pressing the headset button to answer the phone she stood in the center aisle poised with pen and paper ready to write. For the next 20 minutes, every five minutes, the phone vibrated and Karen took down more instructions from her daughter. Not only was Amelia's checklist finally checking off, but it was also producing a complex choreography of short jaunts and little stops all over town. By the fourth call Karen stopped in the snack shop, ordered a soft pretzel and a medium cola so she could sit at a table and plot her course.

"Where are you now?" she asked Amelia.

"I'm at home picking up Zeke and putting away my dry cleaning."

"When are you meeting Jojo?" Karen asked. Again, the name rattled Amelia's thought process.

"3:00, though I'm sure it won't matter if I'm a little late."

"Honey, we need to be leaving at 4pm. We have to be at the airport two hours in advance for international flights," she reminded her daughter. Amelia winced at the seriousness with which her mother regarded the rules.

"Okay, I'll get there on time. The visit will only take about 15 minutes, I'm sure," Amelia stretched. Karen winced on the other end of the call knowing it wouldn't be so short. Only by Amelia's standards could the visit happen in 15 minutes. Miguel Alvarez would have a different agenda.

"Okay," Karen knew it was fruitless to argue with her hard-headed daughter, "I'll drop this stuff at the front desk so you can add it to your suitcase." She paused. "You are packed and ready to go except for this stuff?"

"Of course," Amelia lied, pulling out luggage from the walk-in closet in her bedroom.

"Good." Karen could still tell when her daughter was fibbing. "I'll be there in an hour." Amelia checked her watch. She gave herself 20 minutes to pack in order to miss her mom, so she could deliver Zeke and Binga to their caretakers, and still get to the appointment on time.

"Okay, Mom, that'll be great. Thanks so much. What would I do without you?" Amelia poured all of her make-Mom-happy language into the receiver.

"Miss your flight," Karen joked and ended the call without the usual 'love you, bye'.

Amelia's formula for packing was to put everything on the bed she thought she might like to take arranged by color, event and temperature. Then she would remove half and find that she was well prepared for her trip. Today she had no time to calculate the variables. She grabbed two of everything from every drawer, from each end of the hanging clothes in the closet, and the shoe racks, and piled it into the two bags. She emptied her bathroom vanity into three plastic zipper bags to protect her clothes from high altitude leaks and threw in her brush, blow dryer, and power adapter. The rest would arrive via her mom. She zipped the bags closed, laid her tickets on top, and grabbed Zeke and his favorite squeaky toy before adding her keys and purse to her clenched fists. Grabbing the doorknob she pulled and walked through the doorway into the narrow hall outside her condo.

*Binga!* She realized she was missing the bird and stuck her foot between the door and the frame before they could connect. "Okay, slow it down a bit," she said aloud checking her watch. "It doesn't help if you miss a major piece at this point." She set Zeke down on the floor and grabbed his leash from the bookshelves near the door.

Amelia stacked Zeke's toy and her keys inside her purse and pulled it onto her shoulder. She took Binga's special food from under the sink and added it to her bag. Retrieving her cell phone she called the front desk and asked for her car to be brought up. Amelia emptied Binga's water dish, and returned it to the cage, then grabbed the wire handle and guided the cage to her side. There was more than one thing she had almost missed.

"We have to be more careful." She said to Zeke who was jumping at the door. Amelia threw her overstuffed purse over her shoulder, and opened the door allowing Zeke to bolt down the hallway knowing he would wait at the elevator. For a moment she paused, holding the door open with her hip, searching her mind to make sure she had everything she needed. *I think that's everything.* She let the door close and followed Zeke to the elevator.

Amelia glanced at her watch. It was two o'clock, she was sure she could make it on time.

*Pause, pause, pause...*

# 7

## *Dreaming Duets*

Miguel paced the floor of his South Avondale home. The naturally dark woodwork matched his mood. His call had come too late and Joseph had already left for the day. Alicia had called all of his friend's houses and even some of his cousins but no one had seen him.

Miguel didn't like the idea of facing the lawyer without the boy she had come to see. He wasn't entirely sure the boy was even okay given the temperament of Darius Lovelle and his propensity for revenge. Miguel was really beginning to worry.

"Did you check the pool?" he asked Alicia for the third time.

"Yes. They said they would call if he showed up, but he didn't take his suit."

"I'm going to drive around the block." He grabbed his keys and headed toward the door then called to Alicia, "Let me know if he shows up." He slammed the door as he left. Miguel knew Joseph

139

didn't comprehend the danger he could be in. Miguel refrained from telling his kids anything that might scare them too much, sometimes even when they needed to be scared. He could see how much the kids had already been hurt, and he believed himself capable of protecting them.

*Damn!* Miguel thought, *I should have warned him.* The feeling of urgency that had been following Miguel all morning was growing in his chest.

Pulling away from the curb Miguel began cruising and searching down every alley in South Avondale. Occasionally druggies would start to approach his slow moving vehicle before they recognized the city plates and backed off.

*Any other day,* Miguel dared them to try to sell him weed when he wasn't already occupied. He wished he had asked Alicia what t-shirt Jojo was wearing as he found himself checking out every color of t-shirt he saw.

No kids in Miguel's care were allowed to wear the white t-shirts dawned by most of the neighborhood males. It was a strategy to make everyone look the same, hence nondescript. Ask any victim of crime what the attacker was wearing in South Avondale and the answer would always be, "white t-shirt, baggy pants." For that reason, baggy pants weren't allowed in Miguel's house either.

By the third trip around the block Miguel was completely frustrated. He picked up his cell phone and dialed headquarters.

"District 2, Detective Green." Miguel was relieved his best friend answered the phone.

"Hey Nick. It's Miguel," he started, "have you heard of anything going down in South Avondale?"

"No, why?" Nick asked.

"I was just checking." Miguel wasn't ready to admit he'd lost the kid, even to his best friend. "I'm looking for angles on the Lovelle case," he gave a good excuse.

"He's out. That's all I know."

"Yeah, I know." Miguel hated what he considered always too low bail on assault cases.

"Sorry Miguel. Something will turn up soon."

"Thanks. Keep an eye on it, okay?"

"Sure thing. Where can I find you?"

Miguel looked at his watch. It was 2:30. He decided it would be better, though not easy to be home in case the lawyer showed up early. "I'm heading home. I have a meeting with Jojo's guardian at three."

"What fun!" Nick's tone reflected their mutual history of frustration with lawyers.

Miguel snapped his cell phone closed. He thought about calling the lawyer to postpone the meeting but decided against it. He hoped to see Jojo walking up the front steps when he got home. That was the best he could do.

*Pause, pause, pause...*

"Turn left onto Northrup Avenue..." Amelia made the turn from Vernon Avenue as she obeyed the curt tone of the woman's voice on the GPS receiver stuck to the inside of her windshield. She kept thinking of the unusual way Zeke acted when she dropped him off at the kennel.

Usually Zeke was so happy to see his friends Sherry and Jill who were so wonderful with him. But today he clawed at the gate to his doggie suite and cried when she turned to leave. She had tried to console him, but Zeke had become more frantic the closer she got to the door. It was as if he didn't want her to leave.

Binga also threw a fit at the pet store even though she usually loved to visit with the other birds. By the time Amelia got to the front door the little bird had thrown such a fit feathers were literally flying from her cage.

"5001," the GPS reminded Amelia as she scanned *4997, 4999,*

*5001.* Though it seemed impossible, she thought the address sounded familiar. Amelia saw the 1920's craft house on a small hill and looked for a parking spot. On the sidewalk a foursome of men in white t-shirts were checking out her SUV. *Surely, they can't think I'm here to see them,* Amelia thought, unaware of how many cars from her community regularly cruised the street corner dealers in this and many other neighborhoods like it.

Amelia pulled over and parked in front of the address. The houses were in good shape. That surprised Amelia given the reputation of the neighborhood surrounding the local children's hospital.

Picking up her cell phone Amelia thought to call her mom one last time before she went in to see her young client. "Mom, where are you?"

"At home. What can I get for you now?" Karen Bradford was sorting through her new finds from the days shopping and choosing what to take on the trip.

"Nothing. I just wondered if you could call over to Sherry and Jill's and see if Zeke is calming down. He was really acting strange."

"What do you need me to do if he's not?" Karen couldn't believe the way Amelia coddled the dog.

"Just leave a message on my cell so I know before they close, that's all."

"Okay. Anything else?"

"Not right now," Amelia chortled. "I'm turning off my cell, so I'll call you when I leave."

"Okay. Tell Jojo I said hi," Karen requested as she heard the line go quiet.

Amelia looked up to the porch of 5001 Northrup and saw a tall man she assumed to be Detective Alvarez standing with a boy in a white t-shirt.

*That must be Jojo.* She picked up the name her mother used.

Amelia pulled on the door handle and locked the car using the remote as she slung her briefcase strap over her shoulder. Crossing the street, she squinted into the sunlight and waved hello to the pair on the porch. If they stayed outside, a brief visit would be much more likely.

*Pause, pause, pause...*

Miguel Alvarez looked into the eyes of the young boy on his porch trying to ascertain if he was telling the truth. "You're sure?" he asked. "You haven't seen him anywhere?"

"No," the boy sounded impatient. "Can I go now?" Miguel marveled at how much the too young boy already sounded like the dealers he usually questioned on the street.

"Sure, okay." Miguel looked down at the street and saw the foursome in white shirts. He watched as they spread out and started to run almost before he heard the sound of screeching tires coming around the corner three houses away.

Miguel's eyes locked on the window of a long dark Camaro that had come around the corner and was slowing down in front of his house. The mirrored glass window was sliding down into the door panel. Miguel saw the flash of the gun barrel at the same time he saw who he knew must be the lady lawyer. The sound of bullets splicing the air was in rhythm with the bounding steps of the lawyer as she mounted the stairs waving her hand in a friendly gesture.

While every muscle in Miguel's body that had a connection with survival flexed and pushed the small boy to the wooden porch, the lady lawyer seemed to be oblivious to the danger that was rolling by behind her. The barrel of the semi-automatic AK-47 started broadcasting bullets across Miguel's front yard as the car cruised by in slow motion.

"Get down!" Miguel yelled. As Amelia looked into Miguel's eyes, a growing look of concern shot across her face. She felt a sharp pain between her shoulder blades and the concern turned to shock. The steps started spinning beneath her feet. She turned as she fell to the concrete, landing on her back as she looked into the open window of the Camaro and closed her eyes.

Bullets whizzed past Amelia's body on the steps toward Miguel and the boy on the porch hitting the screen door of the house. Miguel was helpless to do anything but stay on top of the boy to further protect him. In the smattering of 10 seconds the attack was over and Miguel raised his head from the ground. Expecting to see the aftermath of the shooting, Miguel saw only white. He blinked his eyes and tried to focus on the misty fog that surrounded him.

"Holy Shit!" Miguel heard a familiar voice, and turned his head to focus on the curly redheaded lawyer lady he'd last seen in his front yard. She looked at him in amazement. "I was shot!" she exclaimed.

Miguel jumped to his feet checking for the boy he had been covering but he was gone. He peered deep into the mist for signs of the white t-shirts or the Camaro but saw no one other than himself and Amelia in the fog.

*Am I dead?* he wondered, resisting a temptation to make the sign of the cross over himself.

"Not exactly." Another voice came from the fog as a tall elephant moved into view.

"Hrim!" Amelia gasped, "Hrim, I've been shot!"

"Thank goodness," Hrim replied as the fog revealed his entire towering countenance.

"Thank goodness?" Amelia looked stunned as she checked her body for signs of blood. She noticed the gold lamé shoes were on her feet again. *Oh, that's what was missing,* she thought, *I should have known.*

"Tough gaining consciousness in a non-lucid dream," Hrim commented.

Looking up Amelia resumed the exchange with Hrim. "What do

you mean 'thank goodness'? Can't you see? I've been shot!"

"No, I don't see, but I don't doubt it. Word has it you took quite a few of those little silver babies." Amelia's head cocked as if she couldn't quite believe what the elephant was telling her. "I'm just happy you now know what's going on."

"What the hell *is* going on?" Miguel looked at Amelia and the elephant incredulously.

"Oh, I'm sorry," Hrim replied, "This is just your second lucid moment in this whole scenario. How can I help you?"

Miguel stared at the talking elephant and the lady lawyer about whom he felt an incredible sense of déjà vu'. Miguel reached for the gun in the holster under his right arm but it was not there.

"Sorry Miguel." The elephant knew his name. "There are a few things you need to catch up on before we can allow you to play with firearms. But first I would like to get out of this whacky get up."

Hrim looked at Amelia who seemed perplexed. That moment of doubt about what she was seeing was all Hrim needed to melt down into the personage of a very old, bald man wearing a white robe and sandals.

"Hiram?!" Amelia gasped. A part of Miguel seemed to know the old man as well.

"Hrim is fine. Hiram was just an adaptation to the Main Street dream sequence."

"You're not an elephant?"

"No, that's just how you expect to find me now when you enter the fog." A staff materialized in Hrim's waiting hand. "Thanks for releasing me from that illusion. It will make our talk a little easier." Hrim tapped the staff on the ground and a boulder appeared through the mist.

"Pull up a rock and have a seat," Hrim invited. Two more boulders appeared in the fog. Hrim was amused at the images Amelia and Miguel agreed upon as appropriate for some transcendental instruction.

"Miguel," Hrim began, "Do you understand that you have been here before?"

"Where?" Miguel shrugged and looked into the fog. Hrim waved his staff into the mist and the scene began to shift like images in a slide show fading from one to another. Miguel and Amelia watched as Hrim played all of the major scenes from the dreams that preceded his arrival in the fog. In reverse sequence he started with the circus scene and Jojo sparring with the clown. From there the scenes melted rapidly through scenes in small town America to scenes in India. Miguel could see Jojo and Amelia ascending the mountain on the back of an elephant. Then the images flipped wildly forward and he saw the last scene before he landed in the fog - Amelia struck by a bullet in front of his house.

"But that was real," Miguel said. "She was shot!" He looked at Amelia with questioning eyes. "I do remember," he said. "You're Karen Bradford's daughter, the lawyer. But it didn't stop there. I've been working your case. You're in ICU." He looked at Hrim. "How can she be in ICU and here at the same time? Look at her." Miguel stood up and walked over to Amelia, "There's nothing wrong with her!"

"Do you remember the rest?" Hrim ignored the questions about Amelia's health.

"How am I doing?" Amelia interrupted touching Miguel's sleeve.

"Don't answer that question!" Hrim waved his staff and silenced the pair. They looked at him and waited. "You humans need to understand that where you focus your attention is what will be manifest. What is important now is not Amelia's prospects for survival as you have perceived them in the 3-D dream, but what you will accomplish in this dream to bring about the appropriate conclusion."

"What do you mean? I'm dreaming right now?" Miguel tried to balance his lucid state against having a conversation with an elephant turned little old man.

"Yes. You and Amelia and several others have just completed a dream that reviewed everything that occurred during the day leading up to your encounter with the black Camaro," Hrim replied.

"You were there?" Amelia asked.

"Not exactly." Hrim clarified, "All that has occurred so far is a matter of public record."

"The report I filed at the station," Miguel nodded knowingly.

"No, the Akashic," Hrim explained. "The actions of everyone, every thought, every intention, every fear, every ah-ha are recorded in the Akashic. I have tapped into your records and those that are connected to yours. This is how I know what has transpired."

"Then tell us why all that happened," Amelia urged Hrim, half knowing the answer he would give her.

"Can't tell you more than you already know," Hrim explained, "for me, it's out of bounds."

"For you?" Miguel heard the qualification.

"Yes, I cannot bring the knowledge of the Akashic to you, but you may seek after it for yourselves." The whole Wizard of Oz parallels in her dream came up for Amelia as if fresh. She felt like Dorothy finding out that the wizard wasn't a wizard at all and couldn't do anything to get her home. She imagined Hrim floating away in a big hot air balloon and was startled when she heard Miguel.

"Hey! Come back here!" Amelia brought her attention back to the fog and saw Hrim floating off against a sky of blue in a beautiful hot air balloon. Catching herself, Amelia focused her attention on the balloon and imagined it was moving closer to her. The balloon followed her imaginings. Amelia was impressed. The balloon began to float away again. Amelia focused her attention once more on simply seeing the balloon landing in front of her. In a moment Hrim was disembarking the basket and joined Amelia and Miguel on the boulders.

"That was pretty neat." Amelia was impressed with her feat of magic.

147

"Not magic," Hrim corrected. "Intention and manifestation. This is the page we need the two of you on together."

Miguel looked at Amelia who had seemed so pretentious and demanding on the phone. He couldn't quite reconcile the young woman sitting across from him as the same person.

*Pause, pause, pause...*

*Dreams are tricky things. While humans are becoming increasingly aware that they are constantly dreaming, few have begun to understand the subtle nuances of the dream. Without good working knowledge of the different classes and qualifications of dreaming, and most importantly, how to gain control of their dreams, humans endure entire lifetimes of thinking dreams just happen beyond their control, without intent, and mostly for their amusement.*

*Dream Guides maintain a high level of job security as the human race moves at a snail's pace which is, we'll admit, faster than the pace of a royal elephant when calculating for body mass, in uncovering the secrets of their dream habits while continuing to maintain one hell of a nightmare overall. Nevertheless, it is the sacred responsibility of Dream Guides when encountered by lucid dreamers to attempt to explain the practices and processes into which they have entered whether intentional or accidental.*

*Resume, resume, resume...*

"The dreamer perceives and interprets energy according to his or her belief system." Hrim read Miguel's thoughts. "In the earlier dreams, the ones before the dream of the 3-D experience, you did not know who Amelia was, Miguel. You might have been attracted to her dream because of your connection to her case in the 3-D dream. However, it is also likely that you were attracted to her dream

148

because of your connection to Jojo."

Amelia remembered Jojo's disappearance from the circus dream and realized the boy she saw on the front porch with Miguel was not Jojo. "Where is he?" Amelia asked, again knowing the answer before Hrim spoke it.

"Out of bounds," Hrim confirmed. Miguel suddenly felt filled with rage.

"Where is he?" Miguel demanded. "What have you done with him?" Again, Miguel reached for the holstered pistol that was not there.

Hrim understood Miguel's concern and tried to reassure him. "The boy is having his own dream." Hrim pointed to the rock behind Miguel. "Please sit down and let's stop delaying our work. There is much to be done." Miguel stepped back and sat stiffly on the rock.

"I'm responsible for him," Miguel muttered.

"Yes, I know. So let's get on with it." Hrim started again to explain manifesting to the pair when Amelia interrupted him.

"Excuse me Hrim, but I think you're taking a bit too much time yourself and there are some points I think I can fill in that will help Miguel get the big picture." Miguel was surprised at the familiarity with which Amelia addressed him. Hrim motioned with his open palm upward as if to surrender the podium to Amelia. A sparkle of energy ran through Amelia as she felt empowered for the first time since she's come through the fog.

"Right now, I think we're in my dream." She explained, "People move their dreams in and out of other people's dreams as circumstances attract or repel them like little magnets." She looked at Hrim who nodded his head.

*Not bad,* Hrim thought to Amelia. She checked Miguel to see if he had any reaction to the thought exchange. He did not.

"I think this is my dream because the first time I realized I was dreaming I was in a foggy scene like this one. This is how I start a lucid dream, with fog and Hrim."

"And me." Zeke plodded out of the fog and jumped his feet up onto Amelia's knees. He reached to lick her cheek as she dropped down and put her hands around his head and scratched his ears. She looked at Miguel who was apparently stunned to see and hear a talking dog.

"Sometimes animals talk. Sometimes they're not really animals." She smiled at Hrim. "Sometimes you can hear thoughts." She smiled. "I'm okay Zeke, do you feel better now?"

"I thought I'd go nuts at the kennel trying to warn you," Zeke replied. "You don't listen so well in the waking dream."

"You're right, I don't. How's everything going for you?"

"I'd be better if you'd quit screwing around and get me outta' that place. There's a crazy Chihuahua chick who thinks I should be her man! She's driving me crazy and practically blinding me with her rhinestone studded collar!"

"Mom hasn't picked you up?" Amelia looked concerned.

"I think that's close enough." Hrim interjected. "Zeke, why don't you go get a treat, like a good dog?"

"I can't argue wit' 'dat!" Zeke licked his chops and looked back at Amelia and admonished her as he toddled into the fog. "Don't stay out all night!"

Amelia returned her attention to Miguel as Zeke followed a trail of treats into the fog. "People come and go so strangely around here." Amelia played upon her ongoing Oz theme only to realize that neither Hrim nor Miguel seemed to share the same appreciation for the movie classic. She refocused on exploring dream states with Miguel.

"In my last dream, the one where I came to your house, I wasn't lucid. It was a sleeping dream where I wasn't in control of my circumstances the way I was just now with the hot air balloon. In that last dream, in addition to you, I dreamed my step-sister, an employee, my ex-fiancé," she paused to make sure she hadn't missed anyone, "and my mother." Miguel made mental note of the potential suspects and remembered his call to Nick in his own dream.

"From what I've learned so far," Amelia went on, "we walk around thinking 3-D life is different from dreaming but it's not. We also think it's happening to us but it really happens through the power of our imaginations." Miguel watched Amelia skeptically as she stood up from her seat on the rock and paced as if she was presenting a case to a jury.

"So, were you dreaming me or was I dreaming you?" he inquired.

"Yes." Amelia employed an answer she learned from Tetta. "Both ways because everything appears differently based on the viewing point. I was dreaming you from my experience but you were also dreaming for yourself too." Amelia nodded her head as she deepened her understanding of the process and checked in with Hrim who nodded affirmatively and gave her a little wink.

"Whenever we had similar material in our dreams, we bumped into each other.

"So everything I dreamed doesn't necessarily have something to do with you?"

"Not necessarily." Hrim interjected, "But it is likely that even seemingly unrelated events can shed some light on each other." Miguel understood the interaction of facts and how they could build together into one story.

"So if I'm in your dream now, will I remember it when I wake up?" Miguel asked Amelia who looked to Hrim for new information.

"You are both lucid in this dream which means you will remember it. It also means either of you can take it in any direction. This is why it's so important to get you both on the same page." Hrim looked at Amelia. "Much in the same way as your dream of India attracted Jojo because of Dumbo, and then Jojo made it all about his experiences with Darius. We don't want the dream bouncing all over the place at this late stage in the game."

"What about Darius?" The mention of Darius piqued Miguel's attention.

"That's for me to know and you to find out," Hrim replied.

"Out of bounds." Amelia tried to explain for Miguel.

"But not for very much longer," Hrim nodded. "First you two need to agree on what's next. Then you can exchange information, being careful to understand that doing so may send either of you into the same or a different dream experience."

Amelia looked concerned. "I don't think we should split up."

"That would likely be a good idea," Hrim agreed. "What I can tell you is that because of your experiences there are several forces seeking you out in various dream levels and some of them may intend to cause you harm."

Miguel looked at Amelia. He was trying to sort through the events in the front yard. It wasn't clear to him who was the intended target, himself, Jojo, or maybe even Amelia. He reached under his right arm and felt his holster with gun inside.

"Do bullets hurt in dreams?" Miguel asked.

"If a person dreams themselves dead, no matter what level they dream from, then that person may not awaken unless a stronger dream revives him or her or there is a greater plan." Miguel studied the soft blue aged look of Hrim's eyes. They were honest and caring.

"Did Amelia dream herself dead?" Miguel asked. A little sharp breath could be heard as Amelia inhaled quickly.

"Her present state is in line with her perceptions of what would happen if she came in contact with a bullet." Hrim nodded. "But she is not dead and as you know she has her mother strongly dreaming that she'll live."

"And me?" Miguel asked, "Did I get hit too? Am I dead?"

"No. Not then, not in the dream of your waking history. You continue to sleep as you have every night since the event." Miguel felt relieved and yet sorry for Amelia. "However," Hrim continued, "I must suggest that you get to work. Start comparing notes before daybreak, Miguel, about what you saw. If you go back to the waking dream Amelia may well be left here alone except for the guides.

Guides cannot change a dream sequence. Amelia needs your support as her dream will undoubtedly collide with dreams of those who may mean her harm."

Amelia looked at Miguel. Suddenly she was very grateful he turned out to be a detective.

*Pause, pause, pause...*

At the bedside of her daughter Karen Bradford started awake from her dream. She was exhausted from reliving the experience over and over again. She remembered that last phone call, and the next one from Miguel Alvarez. At first she thought he was calling about Jojo. It was, she thought, both a blessing and very strange that he had been the one to call about Amelia. At times, however, she felt so angry toward the man who had helped her help her students so much, and then had invited her daughter to a drive by shooting. She felt herself biting her lower lip, a habit she had developed to keep herself from saying anything she might regret later.

Rubbing her weary eyes she checked her watch. It was 12:55 am. The hospital staff had given up trying to restrict Karen to visiting hours. She needed to make a life or death decision and she had every right to try every way she could think of to revive her daughter. Removing the breathing apparatus, which seemed to be all that was keeping her alive, was out of the question.

Karen sat back in her chair and felt her back ache from the poor posture she maintained while napping. Detective Alvarez was convinced Amelia had seen the shooter. He was sure she could identify him if she awoke. When pressed for why this had happened, Detective Alvarez was open to myriad possibilities some of which he didn't share with Karen. Karen was not satisfied with his plethora of possibilities. She wanted *the* answer.

Karen stood and stretched and moved to leave the curtained area. If there was one thing that could tear an aging mother away from her daughter it was the pressing down of the bladder upon sitting up.

"I'll be back baby." She observed her daughter's beauty even under the mess of tangled tubes and wires. "And so will you."

*Pause, pause, pause...*

Miguel and Amelia were sitting in a booth toward the rear of a coffee shop downtown. Both had decided coffee was important to keep them awake in their lucid dream so they could plow through the issues together. First, they needed to discern why there was a shooting. Amelia secretly enjoyed the thrilling sense of detective work that was developing. She wasn't, however, thrilled with the fact that her recovery didn't seem to be a part of Miguel's puzzle.

"But isn't it most important to find out who shot me?" Amelia demanded self-righteously.

"Not really," he replied. Miguel was arranging a packet of sugar with blue, yellow and pink packets of various artificial sweeteners, a spoon, fork, knife, and several different containers of flavored coffee cream. *"Who* isn't as important as *why,"* he continued. "See this?" He motioned to the spoon. "That's you. Jojo is the fork and I am the knife."

"Who's the sugar?" Amelia asked not identifying with the shape of the spoon.

"Your mom."

"What does she have to do with anything?"

"You never know," Miguel replied. "Right now she's sitting by your bedside."

"She is?"

"Hasn't left for days."

Amelia felt sad for her mother. Miguel resisted telling Amelia anything further about her condition.

"I must be pretty bad off," Amelia surmised.

"She says you told her you would be home soon," Miguel replied.

Amelia remembered sending out the thought from her mom's Main Street dream.

"Okay," Miguel continued, "your mom's the sugar. Jojo's step-dad is the blue packet. Your ex-boyfriend is the pink stuff."

"How does David get in this?" Amelia looked at the blue and pink packets on the table in front of her remembering the blue and red state shoe debacle. She had told Miguel the entire story about the break-up over the pair of gold lamé shoes at Des Shoe. He had seemed very interested in finding out more than Amelia cared to tell about David.

"I'm just documenting everyone and everything that has come up since we started talking." Miguel shrugged his shoulders. "Like the Irish Crème flavored coffee creamer. That's Nick. I called him about half-an-hour before the drive-by." Miguel was careful to not even use the word shooting as he noticed every time he had used the term Amelia had squirmed uncomfortably squeezing her shoulders together.

"Okay, so Nick's on the table too," Amelia agreed. "Who is the pepper?"

"The driver of the Camaro." Miguel looked at her carefully. "You're sure you never saw him?"

"I don't remember." Amelia shrugged her shoulders. Miguel frowned. "Maybe it's out of bounds?" She looked at Miguel apologetically and asked another question. "Who's the salt shaker?" Her attention fell on the little glass bottle filled with salt mixed with white rice.

"Whoever is in charge of this whole operation."

"You mean like a gang leader?" Amelia was convinced the driver shot at the wrong house. You'd have to be an idiot to do a drive-by on a cop's house. She had not read the referral on Jojo beyond the assault charges. She didn't know about Darius' history with drugs or Jojo's claim that he had made several pick-ups for Darius.

Miguel saw the connection between Darius and David as inextricable. Jojo had led him to the shoe store. He was convinced Darius and David knew each other and was, for the moment, unsure Amelia was ignorant of her ex-boyfriend's possible involvement. The nervousness she described the night of the argument over shoes indicated a possible drug habit but the nervousness in the restaurant whispered of something else.

To Miguel, David seemed more nervous about losing Amelia's money than losing Amelia. He wondered if David was feeling the pressure of owing his dealer and losing the money he needed to pay off a debt. *I'm just going to keep this all under wraps for now,* Miguel thought to himself as he pushed the packet of pink stuff that represented the shoe store owner to the side of the table.

Amelia listened attentively to Miguel's thoughts, trying to comprehend the scene he was describing without having a near violent reaction at the same time. The waitress came to the table with a fresh pot of coffee.

"You folks have been here for awhile," she commented. "I thought this might help you." Amelia followed the hand on the coffee pot over the arm and above the shoulder to the calm dark eyes of Tetta. She leapt from the seat and threw her arms around Tetta's neck hugging her sideways, careful not to burn herself on the pot.

*I missed you!* Amelia thought to Tetta.

*Always here for you.* Tetta chuckled and held Amelia around the waist as they both looked down and watched Miguel as he continued to play with his packets and utensils. *Boys will be boys,* she thought to Amelia who could not conceal her growing resentment that he might implicate her in her own shooting.

*Pause, pause, pause...*

Jahni and Hrim walked around the dark side of the Wait Zone trying to find the drunk that had been showing up throughout the

156

project. He was nowhere to be found. Hrim looked down at his sandaled feet on the grimy cobblestones of the back alley where Jahni had taken him. "What do you say to a cup of latte and a round of Chess?" Hrim asked. Instantly the two were transported to the coffee shop where Amelia and Miguel were comparing notes. It was important for these two to develop a liaison of their own so Hrim and Jahni shifted shapes enough to remain unrecognizable to the pair sitting at the back table. Hrim produced his Coffee Shop credit card at the counter and endured a few seconds of teasing from Jahni.

"Well, well. You certainly are moving into the 21st century," Jahni laughed.

"One of my projects gave it to me in appreciation," Hrim explained. "Might as well use it up." The duo retired to two comfy armchairs. On the table between them, a marble chessboard and pieces awaited play. Jahni advanced his pawn.

"So how do you think this is going to turn out?" Jahni asked nodding to the back table. Hrim considered the possibilities.

"I'd like to say it's too soon to tell, but it really is getting down to the wire." Everything was in a state of flux. Since no one had nailed any of the major pieces into place yet, the entire outcome could be radically different than present circumstances indicated. When it came to the Akashic, Hrim was well experienced in its shifting nature. He knew what he saw now, but if one piece changed, the entire record could be adjusted. History could be re-written long before or after it was initially entered into record.

Even human science had discovered the flexibility of outcome and called it quantum indeterminacy when Erwin Schroedinger had illustrated how a cat could be both dead and alive until human consciousness was superimposed on the subject and made the final determination. The same was true for Amelia. The question remained as to whose consciousness or dream would prevail.

Hrim tipped his head back and sensed to a particular thread in the dream sequence. He opened his eyes and squinted at Jahni. "I'd like to say 'this or something better,' but right now, it could get a lot worse."

Hrim looked across the floor at Tetta who was playing waitress. "Damn. Wouldn't you know it," he grumbled.

"What's up?" Jahni asked moving his rook into position for checkmate.

"Amelia and Miguel are splitting up and things could get messy. Jahni, can you stick with Miguel?" Jahni nodded.

"Good," Hrim continued, "Tetta's with Amelia. I need to check in with Jojo and our buddy Galahad." Hrim started to rise.

"Wait!" Jahni hissed looking incredulously at Hrim. "I almost forgot all about Galahad filling out the snail's shell as Jojo's guide!" Hrim laughed heartily and rejoined Jahni next to the chessboard for a moment.

"That's what happens when your students don't play by the rules, they get assignments that will teach them better." Hrim shook his finger at Jahni.

"You can't hold me responsible for him," Jahni protested. "His ego beat him to the Wait Zone."

"Well, hopefully sliming around as a slug in a shell has taught him a thing or two about taking things into his own hands." Hrim laughed. "Though that acrobatics on the mountainside was a little over the top."

"He was just working with Jojo's imaginings," Jahni insisted.

"Well, right now Jojo is imagining himself on an intergalactic trek in his snail shaped spaceship. I think it's time we bring him in so he can contribute to the clean-up efforts." Hrim shook his head. "I don't think you and I have ever finished a game of chess. Better get ready to follow Miguel. As soon as he realizes Amelia's gone he'll be off and running too."

*Pause, pause, pause…*

158

Tetta monitored thoughts from the counter across the coffee shop as Amelia grew increasingly weary of Miguel's silent belief he was in control of his case which included her life. Amelia searched her mind for a way to have a say in her own rescue. She reviewed what she had learned and found a possible way out of Miguel's dream and back to her own. She believed a phone call could connect her with a different dream based on both the call she took at the theatre and the one which disclosed what she now knew to be Miguel's home address. She also found that spaces were interchangeable between dreams, just as the diner in Main Street America had morphed into the restaurant where she broke it off with David. Amelia decided to initiate her own crossover. She excused herself, leaving Miguel at the table, and went to the Ladies' Room.

Tetta locked in to Amelia's coordinates and sent the message to Hrim just before Amelia wished herself into the bathroom of David's apartment. Outside the apartment in the hallway Tetta slid into the position of cleaning lady and ran the vacuum sweeper over the cheap industrial carpet.

Amelia was pleased that she had been able to morph to the waking dream. She was unclear about a few details that she hoped weren't too important. She heard David's voice in the living room. She didn't hear anyone responding so she crept out of the bathroom through the bedroom hoping to listen in on what she believed was a phone conversation. Peering through the partially opened doorway out of the bedroom through the hall to the living room Amelia watched the back of David's head as she crept closer.

David was standing in the middle of the living room having a conversation with himself.

*I told him he needed to get help,* she thought.

"I think we should just split with what we have," he proposed. David turned his head in the air as if he was listening for a reply.

*He's crazier than I thought.* Amelia moved into the hallway to make sure David wasn't talking to someone on his cell phone.

159

"It's just too close," David sounded as though he was trying to convince himself. "The police have been by three times about what happened to Mimi." David listened as if he was on a headset but Amelia didn't see the characteristic flash of David's Bluetooth in his ear.

"When I pull off this last deal, I'll be able to take care of her the way I always dreamed."

*He's delusional if he thinks I would come back to him.* Amelia wondered if David's conversation with himself was proof that Miguel was right about the drugs.

"Amelia can dump me, but *she* will never leave me." David crossed the living room toward the hallway.

*SHE?* Amelia's eyes widened. *Who's SHE?* Amelia pressed herself against the wall hoping she was right and would be invisible to David.

Oblivious to Amelia's presence, David walked into the bedroom and rolled open the sliding door on the closet. Reaching up he lowered a suitcase down from the shelf and laid it on the bed. Amelia crept closer as David opened the suitcase. Amelia stared at the bundles of money inside then searched David's face for some clue. Could it have come from dealing drugs as Miguel imagined at the coffee shop?

"Between you and me," David cooed to the money, "we'll be able to go far." David closed the suitcase, grabbed it with a triumphant flair, turning a bizarre pirouette before he strode past Amelia into the living room. She heard the front door slam as he left the apartment. Amelia ventured out into the open area of the living room. She opened the door and was engulfed in the roaring vibrations of the vacuum cleaner. Looking into Tetta's scolding eyes, Amelia thought of an excuse. *I needed to see if it was true,* she defended.

"You need to trust Miguel and stay close to him," Tetta urged. "I cannot save you. I'm not allowed to intervene. You need to work together with Miguel while you're both still on the same dream frequency."

"Miguel doesn't even trust me," Amelia argued. "He won't tell me everything he's thinking."

"But you're privileged to his thoughts," Tetta pointed out.

"Yes, and that's what brought me here."

"So what did you learn?"

"I think David is dealing drugs." Amelia still felt surprised. "But it's not with Darius, it's a woman. *Another* woman." She seethed.

"Then you need to share that with Miguel." Tetta surveyed Amelia's energetic structure and felt the resistance growing.

"When I know who she is, I'll let Miguel know." Amelia's ego resisted Tetta's advice and confirmed the energetic wall Tetta perceived.

"Amelia!" Tetta worried that Amelia's resistance would cut off her fledgling connection with Miguel.

"It's my dream," Amelia insisted. "It's my life." She turned and let the door fall closed behind her leaving Tetta in the hallway as she walked to the window and gazed out on the traffic below. "And in case you forgot," Amelia shouted over her shoulder through the door, "visiting Miguel is what got me into this mess."

Tetta listened as Amelia thought of how much she had helped David save his beloved store to establish it as a powerful force in the world of upscale accessories. He didn't need to deal drugs, but he had; and he had betrayed her trust in more than one way. Throughout her entire body Amelia felt complete resistance to trusting any man at the moment.

*I bet he's going to the store. I bet he is running drugs out the back door. I bet I can beat him there.* Amelia glanced at the door as she crossed the living room and headed for the bathroom off David's bedroom.

*Maybe you can.* Tetta psychically argued. *But you should take Miguel with you!*

Unsure if she really needed to be in a similar type of place she imagined herself to the restroom in the stock room at Des Shoe. As the room shifted and became smaller, she was grateful no one was there to greet her. Peeking out through the slightly open door of the small bathroom she imagined sharing the restroom by surprise. *That could get messy,* she thought. *There must be some way to check out the scene before I arrive. I'll ask Hrim next time I see him.*

*Pause, pause, pause...*

Miguel knocked on the Ladies' Room door and heard no response.

"Can I help you sir?" a bus boy stopped to ask.

"I hope so." Miguel pulled his badge from his shirt pocket and flashed it. "My friend went in there awhile ago and now she's not responding. Is there any other exit?"

"No sir." The busboy replied.

"I'm concerned about her health," Miguel lied. "Can you open it?"

"I'll get the key." The bus boy disappeared around the corner. In a moment he returned and unlocked the door to reveal the empty restroom.

"Thanks." Miguel left the busboy holding the door after making sure there were no windows. He felt even more uncertain of Amelia's innocence with her unplanned departure. *A high-powered corporate attorney would be almost invisible to the law as leader of a drug ring*, Miguel considered.

As he returned to the booth, Miguel tied the drive-by to his visit to Des Shoe, but he couldn't be sure who the intended target was. Maybe they intended to wipe out the witness, maybe the cop who was getting too close. If Amelia was involved, maybe someone had rebelled. Maybe she got in the way of the hit she had ordered. After all, she expected Jojo to be home at that time.

He tried a different combination and pushed the pink and blue packets together on the tabletop. Miguel wondered if David Delaney had been contacted after he left the store. Maybe Darius Lovelle had received a call, though the manager seemed far too haughty to be open to someone like him. None of them really felt like a salt or pepper shaker to Miguel's detective senses. Someone, other than just Amelia, was missing from the scene.

In the midst of all this tracking Miguel had become aware of a memory from a dream sequence in Main Street America when he had become lucid the first time. He knew that someone was following them then. Miguel remembered the protective feeling he had for Amelia and Jojo at that moment. Both seemed to be in danger. Even if Amelia wasn't completely innocent, she didn't deserve to die. Miguel renewed his commitment to protect both Jojo and Amelia, and solve the case.

Miguel pondered where Amelia might have disappeared to while Jahni listened in on his thoughts from across the room. The detective was very good at putting pieces together, even if they continued to lead him in more than one direction. At least he wasn't stuck in the wrong direction. Miguel didn't quite know where to begin and he felt a little lost.

Hrim had strongly recommended the pair should stay together. Even though he was considering Amelia as a suspect in her own dream, he had also hoped to benefit from what she knew about the dream process. Miguel figured Amelia knew most of the players better than he did. He decided he needed to find Amelia.

Miguel thought about the way Amelia had sent Hrim floating in the balloon when they first consciously met in the fog. He recalled she said she imagined what she wanted to happen in order for it to come true. Miguel focused on the spoon that represented Amelia. He wished with all his might that Amelia would rejoin him in the booth. Nothing seemed to happen. He continued to focus on the spoon and imagined Amelia's curl framed face until he could see it on the spoon's rounded surface.

Picturing Amelia coming closer and closer to him the spoon suddenly jumped off the table and hurtled toward Miguel smacking him in the forehead. The spoon clattered to the table. Miguel rubbed his smarting forehead and looked around the room to see if anyone had noticed. He caught the eye of a man sitting on a stool at the counter who was laughing at Miguel.

*Would you like a little help?* Jahni thought. Miguel listened to the voice inside his own head. He was sure he had delivered head cases to the psych ward for less realistic hallucinations.

Miguel's eyes locked on Jahni and he replied with thought to test this newfound skill Amelia had described. *Are you talking to me?* Miguel ventured.

*Oh come on, you can do better than that!* Jahni laughed at the impersonation of Clint Eastwood inside Miguel's mind.

Miguel jumped to his feet and stared at Jahni who jumped off the stool and put a reassuring hand on Miguel's long blue shirt sleeve.

"Really, it's okay. I'm here to help. Jahni morphed into the personage of Hrim's brother from Main Street America, and Miguel relaxed a little. I can give you instruction on how to wish yourself where you want to be. You can't make Amelia do anything, but you can follow her." Jahni motioned to the booth and the pair sat down across from each other.

"Here's what you can do," Jahni continued. "Conjure up an image of Amelia. Forget about using the spoon as a focusing tool. You have everything you need in the heart of your imagination." Jahni's voice dropped a note and he began speaking slowly and deliberately as he guided Miguel. "See Amelia's face in your mind's eye. See her hair, her eyes, the way she smiles. Feel Amelia in your heart."

Miguel closed his eyes tentatively yet was immediately deeply entranced by all of the images of Amelia flooding through his mind. He saw her from the moment he had first laid eyes on her helpless body on the steps of his house, with her mother in the hospital, to

164

seeing her in India, at the picnic, during the circus. Miguel had been taking detailed note of her appearance, her quirks, and habits all along. Jahni observed the connection that had now been formed between Miguel and Amelia.

"Now," Jahni said, "let yourself move out through your heart to connect with this energy that is Amelia and when you feel her presence you will find yourself with her."

Miguel opened his eyes to look at Jahni doubtfully, but instead found himself watching Amelia as she peeked out of the bathroom across the stock room at Des Shoe. The door of the rear entrance opened and David walked in.

David immediately started rummaging through the shoe boxes on the shelves in the stock room.

"Dammit!" David swore. "Where did it go?" Amelia watched cautiously from the restroom as he started tossing shoe boxes over his shoulders. As they crashed on the concrete floor behind David, expensive stiletto heels, pricey pumps, and walking shoes popped out and mixed in glistening multi-colored patterns across the floor.

Miguel watched Amelia and tried to listen to her thoughts to see if he could ascertain why she was spying on the man he imagined to be David Delaney.

"There you are!" David stood transfixed with a box cradled in his hands. It was the box for the gold lamé shoes he had urged her to take against her will. She looked down at her feet. The shoes were on tight.

"The perfect fit." David removed the lid and daintily reached in the box to lift the gold lamé shoes by their straps. Setting them gently on the shelf, he turned the box over and shook a folded manila envelope into his right hand.

"I guess it's fate," he cooed at the envelope. "If she had taken the shoes and left, you would be long gone." He lifted the edge of his jacket and tucked the folded envelope in the inside pocket. "You're going to take me and my baby very, very far."

Amelia sneered in disgust for his lusty comment. *Not after I get a hold of you,* she promised. Miguel heard a faint buzz he thought might be Amelia. He tried to tune in by relaxing a little and acting like it was easy to listen to her thoughts.

"All I have to do now is find my little partner in crime." David opened the back door and exited into the alley behind Des Shoe.

*His partner in crime?* Amelia wondered as he turned the key in the lock. "Jojo?"

Miguel heard Amelia's thoughts clearly for the first time and he tried to keep his own thoughts quiet.

*You son of a...* Miguel winced at the volume of Amelia's thoughts. *Damn you!* She continued to shout and Miguel wished he could turn down the volume. Instantly she toned down as she stepped out of the restroom and started stomping across the floor on the high heels of her gold lamé shoes, kicking designer shoes out of her way as she headed for the door.

"How could you do this you twit?" Amelia kicked at a box. "And use a poor little kid?" She scuttled a purple pump into the air with the side of her foot. "I've had about all I can take!" Amelia ranted out loud.

Suddenly a gunshot blasted from the alley. Amelia pulled back her hand that was reaching for the doorknob. Miguel, not understanding their invisible nature, came out of the shadows and grabbed her, quickly placing his hand over her mouth as she struggled to scream for help.

"Shh! Shh! It's Miguel!" he whispered frantically into her ear. Amelia bit him hard on the finger. Miguel didn't know he could feel pain in a dream. Amelia twisted out of his arms and turned to him pulling her hand from his.

"Let me go!" she hissed. Opening the door, Amelia stopped in the frame. The black Camaro was spinning its wheels in getaway mode. On the pavement lay David. Slowly, the life completely emptied from his eyes that were wide open and staring in her direction.

*At least I'm not alone.* Amelia heard David's last thought as Miguel stepped past her to check his vital signs. They were gone.

Pause, sniff, sniff, pause...

## Objects in Mirror are Closer than They Appear

Jahni and Hrim met in the reception area of the Wait Zone as David Delaney crossed over the line. No one had entertained a dream of him living that was stronger than the one that had killed him.

"That's him." Jahni pointed to David. "That's the drunk!"

"Not anymore." Hrim corrected.

David proceeded to the pair looking disheveled and quite disappointed.

"Am I dead?" he asked the twosome.

"Pretty much." Jahni nodded.

"I'm not surprised." David hung his head a moment then looked at them in alarm. "Am I going to hell?"

"Do you think that you should?" Hrim asked. David delved deeply into his Roman Catholic background for an answer.

"I suppose I could, but isn't it payback enough that I'm dead so young?"

"What brings you here?" Jahni asked to see what David would volunteer.

"Fate?" David tried.

"Try again." Hrim gave David the universal upraised eyebrow look of disapproval. "What's your crime?"

"Well, I was heading for my car and this thug crunched me in the head with something hard." David searched between Hrim and Jahni's faces to see if his answer would pass.

"Then what?" Jahni nodded.

"He had a gun and ordered me to empty my pockets."

"What was in your pockets?" Jahni wanted to see if Miguel's drug dealing angle would pan out.

"Nothing." Hrim and Jahni glared at the sheepish grin on David's face. "I mean my wallet, sunglasses." David tried. The pair continued to stare expectantly. David wondered if they knew what he had and were testing him to see if he would be honest.

"An envelope," he offered tentatively. Jahni's eyebrows rose with interest.

"What was in the envelope?" Hrim asked. David hesitated as if he still had something to lose. "You're dead David, what does it matter?" Hrim reminded. "There's not much left to lose except eternity."

"Stuff." David kept it brief.

"Stuff?" Hrim and Jahni repeated. "Was this stuff valuable?"

"In a way," David agreed. "I didn't care about it very much, but it was worth a fortune to others." David's eyes glimmered at the thought of money. Hrim and Jahni silently consulted with one another.

"Where did you get this stuff?" Jahni asked.

"From a friend of a friend." Hrim sighed as David continued to make things difficult. "Listen, I'll tell you what you want to know if you promise I won't have to go to hell," David offered.

"Can't do that." Hrim shook his head. On top of his already dead state, David turned a whiter shade of pale.

"I thought you were in charge." David attempted to find a way to change his situation.

Hrim shook his head. "Saint Peter is taller and usually hangs out at the pearly gates."

"Oh for God—I mean Gosh Sake! What do I need to do to get out of this?" David's eyes darted back and forth between Hrim and Jahni.

Jahni scanned the record. "You should have asked that before you crossed over."

*Pause, pause, pause...*

"Shouldn't you be chasing after the car?" Amelia stood frozen in the doorway.

"On foot?" Miguel fished David's cell phone out of his pocket. "I'm wondering who David might have spoken with in the last 24 hours." He explained as he flipped open the phone and started searching its contents.

"Himself." Amelia remembered David's conversation with himself at the apartment.

"What about this number. It's the same one showing up five times. Do you recognize it?" Miguel held out the phone. Amelia made no effort to see.

"I don't recognize anything right now." Amelia looked down at David's lifeless body. Miguel knew the shock that was setting in by heart. Too many victims' families became worthless for information due to their grief. He sidled between Amelia and David.

"C'mon Amelia, look at this." He held up the cell phone so she could see the numbers. His eyes searched her confused face for some signs of recognition.

Amelia looked at the glowing screen on the phone. There was something familiar about the number, but she couldn't place it.

"I don't get it." She shook her head and turned away from Miguel and the scene at their feet. "None of this makes any sense."

Miguel pressed the send button on the cell phone and waited. The call was answered on the second ring but no one said a word.

"Hello?" Miguel spoke into the phone. "Who is this?" The call disconnected. Miguel snapped the phone shut.

"What did they say?" Amelia asked.

"Nothing. This indicates to me that they didn't expect to hear from David." Miguel put the phone in his pocket. "Did you see the driver or catch any part of the plate?" There was something about the plate that also struck a cord with Amelia but again, she couldn't pinpoint what it was.

"No, sorry. I was really focused on David. I couldn't believe what I was seeing." Amelia's eyes filled with tears. Then the tears turned to something else. She felt as if a huge weight had been placed upon her chest. She opened her mouth and gasped for air but none came in.

"Amelia?" Miguel jumped up from the pavement and rushed to her side. "What's wrong?!" Amelia shook her head and put her hand to her chest.

"I can't," she choked. Amelia sank against Miguel and fell slowly to the ground.

Miguel's thoughts instantly went to Karen Bradford sitting bedside in the hospital. He looked deep into Amelia's eyes and blinking found himself next to Karen in the Intensive Care Unit.

"She's coding!" The nurse hit the alarm calling staff to Amelia's bay on the ICU. Then she firmly grabbed Karen by the shoulders and forced her to turn away from Amelia. "You have to leave."

"No, I can't!" Karen felt herself start to shake as tears distorted her vision. She felt wild inside as if there was something she could do to protect her daughter.

"Did she sign the DNR?" the attending physician asked as he entered the curtained bay.

"She hasn't been able to," the nurse answered.

"Then you must leave Mrs. Bradford so we can do our job." He turned and grabbed the paddles from the crash cart.

As Karen strained to see Amelia through her tears, Miguel realized she could not see him next to the bed. Even so, he tried to achieve eye contact with Karen, and nodded to her in reassurance as the nurse led her away. Miguel moved in closer to Amelia, unaffected by the activity around him. Bending low he whispered into her ear, "You have to stay here for now," he encouraged. "Don't leave us Amelia. We're almost there."

The machine that was monitoring Amelia's heart made a long droning sound and Miguel looked to see the flat line roll across the screen uninterrupted.

"Please Amelia!" Miguel wished for a dream stronger than what he was seeing.

"Clear!" the doctor shouted. Miguel placed his hands around Amelia's hand as the current went through her body and sent him in a wave of energy straight through to the Wait Zone where Amelia was already standing.

"Oh for goodness sake!" Tetta practically swore. "You too?" Amelia and Miguel looked at each other. "Listen you both need to go back, it's not your time yet!" Tetta implored impatiently.

"Are you sure?" Amelia asked.

"It could have been, but things have changed, now get back! Both of you!"

*Pause, pause, pause...*

Miguel woke up feeling as if he hadn't slept all night. He clearly remembered all of his dreams and shot out of bed to begin determining what was real and what might have been the embellishments of his imagination.

Miguel remembered the shooting behind Des Shoe and turned on the morning news to see if it was true. He impatiently endured hearing that the day was supposed to be sunny with the possibility of afternoon showers.  When the weather report finished Miguel found no news of a shooting or the slain store owner.

Miguel grabbed the phone and dialed the seven numbers he knew could lead him to the solution.

The cell phone vibrated on the end table beside the bed.  Nick Green picked it up and checked the number lighting up on the screen before he answered.

"I can't golf today." Nick answered the phone.

"Nick, have you heard anything about a shooting last night at Des Shoe?"

"What?"  Nick's grogginess was quickly cleared away as Miguel urgently jumped to the point.

"The owner of Des Shoe was shot last night."

"How did you hear?" Nick pushed up on his elbow. "I was finishing a case late last night when the call came in.  Robbery, I think."

"Nick, it's not robbery," Miguel's voice was low and steady.

"No?  What ya' got partner?" Nick was interested by Miguel's inside knowledge. "No names have been released." He sat up on the edge of the bed letting his toes lightly touch the bare wood floor.

"It has to do with that drug case... Darius Lovelle, the boy." Miguel paused, "All of it Nick.  I need your help."

"Where and when?" Nick replied without hesitation.

"I'm stuck at home until Alicia arrives.  Can you meet me here?"

"Sounds like a plan."

"Thanks Nick."

"No problem," Nick reassured his former partner.  "I'll be there within the hour."  Nick hit the disconnect button. The blanket on the bed next to him squirmed.

"Who was that?" a soft hand touched Nick's bare shoulder.

"Nothing.  Just something I need to take care of," Nick replied.

"But you said you could take off.  It's Sunday!" the cuddling lump complained.

"Don't worry, I'll be back before you're up.  Now go back to sleep." Nick kissed the top sheet of the form that squeezed up against him. Sitting of the edge of the bed and pulling on his pants Nick wondered how Miguel had apparently gotten himself so deep into this.

*Pause, pause, pause...*

Amelia looked past Tetta and saw David talking with Hrim and Jahni.

"I'll go," she promised, "in a minute." She walked past Tetta and approached David.

"Mimi?" David seemed surprised. "Did you die too?"

"Only for a moment," Amelia nodded to Jahni and Hrim then turned back to David. "I'm sorry about your loss of life," she said softly.

"Thanks." He paused, wondering what more appropriate response he could express upon receiving sympathy over his own demise, then added, "I guess."

"David, I just want to know how you could use a little boy to deal drugs, and how you could cheat on me."

"What?" David was speechless.

"I was there David. I heard and saw everything. I saw the money, I heard you talking about *her*. Who is she?" Amelia crossed her arms emphatically.

"Mimi, I didn't cheat on you." David looked pleadingly at Hrim thinking one man ought to help another.

"But you went on and on about giving *her* what *she deserved*." Amelia quoted with her fingers in the air as she quoted David. "How can you tell me there was no other woman?"

David looked hard at Amelia and then to Hrim. "If I tell her the truth, do I get brownie points?" Hrim scanned the ethers for the connection only David could make now that he had been asked directly for historical information about himself that pertained to Amelia.

175

"Yes, that would help you move on." Hrim nodded.

"Okay," Amelia felt validated, "who was the *she* you wanted to take care of with your illegally gotten gains?" Fists firmly planted on her hips Amelia was in lawyer mode. She was ready to win, but not ready to lose.

"I'm sorry Mimi." David's voice broke off as he thought of the one true love he would never be able to take care of as he had dreamed, "Trisha and I..."

As David began Amelia felt herself reeling backward as if she was hurtling through time. David and Hrim, Jahni and Tetta disappeared from her view. Suddenly she found herself sitting not in the fog of a lucid dream, but under the fog of unconsciousness. The paddles burned through her skin and she could hear the beeping of her heart on the monitor. For a moment she thought she was going to stay, then everything went black again.

*Pause, pause, pause...*

Miguel tried to convince himself that Amelia was all right. He had only a vague recollection of the woman who sent them back. Sitting by the phone he picked up the handset and dialed the number for the ICU.

"She coded this morning." The ICU desk nurse was accustomed to Miguel's calls for daily updates. The pause after her statement was more than Miguel could bear.

"Is she okay?" he pleaded.

"She remains in critical condition, but they did revive her."

"Breathing?" Miguel asked.

"By respirator," the nurse replied. How Amelia managed to stay alive didn't matter as much to Miguel as simply knowing that she was alive.

"Thank you." Miguel replaced the handset in its cradle.

Miguel decided not to wake Jojo. He wasn't sure what his

reasoning was. Something just told him to wait and he was trying to be more sensitive to the subtle influences that might be around him.

Having discovered his own invisibleness at Amelia's bedside, Miguel wondered why it was that only in the waking dream did he or Amelia appear to be non-apparent. *Perhaps,* he thought, *we limit our perceptions when we think we're awake. We don't think dreams are real, so we don't allow ourselves to perceive anything other than our so-called reality. We can't see what's right in front of our noses sometimes.* More pertinent thoughts hadn't been imagined during the course of the dream sequences.

Miguel looked up and saw Nick's tall figure on the porch through the curtained front door. Walking through the dining room he crossed the entry area and opened the door to his old friend.

Nick and Miguel had entered the force together 15 years earlier. They had been partners for ten years before Miguel made detective and Nick stayed on the beat. It had been a tough break for Nick. He almost didn't stay on the force after the Lovelle shooting incident. Nick was on desk duty for a year before they let him back in the community. Miguel never had a partner like Nick again. He was the most in-depth analyst Miguel knew and the only one he believed could help him piece together the puzzle.

"You look wasted." Nick observed Miguel as he shook his hand and closed the door behind himself.

"It's been a long and busy night." Miguel ran his hand through his dark hair.

"So tell me what got you involved in the Delaney shooting? I didn't know you were there last night."

"I wasn't," Miguel lied, wondering if he could tell Nick about the dream experience. "Not *really.*" He decided he didn't have time to explain how he knew what he did. Carefully he laid out the connections between Jojo, Darius, and the missed pick-up at the back of the store which had gotten Jojo removed from Darius into his custody. Miguel shared his speculation that Darius was using Jojo to run drugs and that David had lived out his usefulness to the operation.

"So I think his own people whacked him last night," Miguel finished.

"Not bad." Nick looked out the window across the dining room table. "Not bad at all." He looked at Miguel. "So who do you figure is behind it all?"

"I'm not sure, but a black Camaro was at the store last night. Same as the one that drove by the house last week. I'm certain it's the same shooter."

Nick studied Miguel. How could he know so many of the details of the shooting without being directly involved? What witness could have let Miguel know of the Camaro connection?

Miguel looked at Nick blankly. "Got any ideas?" he asked again for help. Miguel was tracing imaginings of the condiment arrangement from the coffee shop on his dining room table. He hoped Nick would be able to help him figure out who the salt and pepper shakers were.

*Pause, pause, pause...*

Amelia noticed small pinpoints of light permeating the darkness that had enveloped her. She moved her head and noticed more and more white glowing dots before her eyes.

"Isn't it cool?" Amelia heard a familiar voice to her right. She looked but saw no one. The voice continued, "Millions and zillions of stars fill the large format screen mounted in the intergalactic snailing vessel the S.S. Gala-Galahad!"

"Snailing vessel?" Amelia searched. "Jojo, is that you?"

A red strobe light started flashing and Amelia could see that she was sitting at a control panel next to Jojo looking at a television screen that was apparently showing them the scene outside the vessel. The vessel was shaped in a spiral.

"Where are we?" Amelia felt a little slimy.

"Sir Galahad." Jojo had been practicing.

"It looks like Dumbo. Though I've never been inside a snail before and wouldn't know how to tell for sure."

Jojo ducked his head low and motioned for Amelia to come close so he could whisper in her ear. "It is Dumbo but he wanted to change his name so now he's Sir Galahad. Okay?"

"Okay," Amelia whispered back. "Jojo, where are we?" She continued to whisper.

"Oh, you don't have to whisper anymore," Jojo whispered. Standing up and pointing his finger high in the air, Jojo took a deep breath and shouted, "We are snailing through the universe!"

The red strobe light continued to flare and Jojo pushed a button on the instrument panel to shut it off. Jojo shrugged his shoulders. "It goes off every hour and I can have an intergalactic battle if I want, but I have to focus," he explained.

"What happens if you don't focus?" Amelia asked, half afraid she was about to be involved in some wild spaceship sparring.

"The bad guys don't come and I don't win. That's all. Computer," Jojo called out. "Lights!" he commanded. The snail shell became softly illuminated.

"How do you know how to do all this?" Amelia asked, forgetting the power of a child's imagination.

"It's easy. Whatever I want can happen here," Jojo replied.

The back of the snail undulated under Amelia as the body made way for the head of the snail to come inside the shell.

"Well, Miss Amelia!" Sir Galahad exclaimed. "Bloody good to see you!" The snail donned a pair of silver aviator goggles on its head even as the gigantic tubular eyes continued to ogle her from a towering distance.

The snail shifted to a country accent running through various personas of Saturday morning adventure films. "Where to, little lady?"

In seconds the snail had gone from 007 to the Duke. Amelia

wasn't sure who would come up next. The question of where she wanted to go brought the most recent piece of information back to her memory.

She remembered David had been involved with Trisha and that news had apparently made her fade through resuscitation into Jojo's dream. Apparently the enemy she kept close had gotten too close – to her boyfriend.

She couldn't understand why they were apparently buying and selling drugs out of Des Shoe. She looked at Jojo. At the very least she would have thought better of either David or Trisha than to believe they would involve and endanger a young boy.

It occurred to Amelia that Trisha must have suspected Jojo could get David in trouble and that David might reveal her involvement as well. The black Camaro fell into place, the letters on the plate now read clearly in her mind: Lady Law. The phone number was Trisha's. She imagined Trisha could be ruthless enough to eliminate David, but hurting a boy still seemed outrageous even for Trisha. *Then again,* she pondered, *maybe the shooting wasn't directed at Jojo. Maybe she* wanted *to have me shot...or Miguel.*

"Look Miss Amelia!" Jojo was pointing to the large-format viewing screen, oblivious to Amelia's concerns. Amelia looked at the screen to observe the colorful dust of a star being born.

"That's beautiful," she acknowledged. "Jojo?"

"Yes ma'am?" There was something okay about young children using the term.

"Do you remember Miguel?"

"Detective Alvarez?" Amelia was surprised Jojo seemed to know who Miguel really was.

"Yeah, that's him."

"He's a friend of my teacher. I'm staying with him because my step-dad is in trouble again."

"Darius?" Amelia clarified.

"Yeah, that's him." Jojo busied himself by pushing buttons and

whirring gadgets on the panel filled with blinking lights before him.
"Well, you're right." Amelia tried to keep Jojo engaged, "Your
dad is in trouble."

"Step dad," Jojo corrected.

"Yes," Amelia agreed, "and I'm afraid Miguel might be in trouble
too. I'm thinking I need to go and try to help him." Jojo looked up
with renewed enthusiasm.

"That sounds cool." Jojo started flipping switches on the control
panel inside the snail, "I'll turn this baby around and get you there in
no time!"

Amelia wasn't planning on taking Jojo along, but now faced with
Jojo attempting to enact a rescue through his potentially erratic
dream on the snailing vessel, she felt a need to convince him to join
her dream. She tilted her head back and attempted to access the
Akashic to see what was going on. Unfortunately her new skills
failed to yield much information. All she could access was faint
memories of old Star Trek programs. She decided what she needed
could be drawn from the snailing vessel theme.

"Jojo, I think we need to beam down to Miguel's house and make
sure everything is alright." She gave it a try.

"Awesome!" Jojo closed his eyes and imagined a transporter
room which instantly materialized inside the snail.

"Wait a minute, what about me?" Sir Galahad looked
disappointed.

"You wait here and keep a tractor beam on us," Jojo ordered
without missing a beat. "If I need you, I'll call you." Jojo patted his
left chest as if he had a communicator button implanted in his shirt.

"Call me at the least hint of trouble?" the snail asked.

"Promise! Now beam us down so I can get back in time to watch
some Japanese Anime!" Jojo and Amelia climbed into the
transporter stalls and a button on the instrument panel mysteriously
depressed starting a spiral of glittering lights to fill the stalls around
Jojo and Amelia.

"We're off to save Miguel and the future of our planet!" Jojo jumped into a superhero stance next to Amelia and their bodies disappeared into the flurry of sparkling lights.

*Pause, pause, pause...*

Shima always thought it was the poverty of India that produced its mystical experiences and understanding as some sort of distracting compensation for the suffering reality of so many of its dreamers. Like most children, Shima was a master of lucid dreaming at an early age. As a survival skill it had suited her well over the years. Using it to track the other players in the plot over the course of the past year had proven to be very beneficial.

Shima thought about the money she felt she deserved. She felt she deserved *him* too. He was the real mastermind, not Trisha. He had arranged the connections to move the packages and bring in the money for her, but Shima was convinced Trisha didn't really love him. From the day she met him, Shima felt competitive with Trisha for his affection. Her job at Des Shoe made it necessary for them to include her and kept her inside the loop. When Amelia broke up with David, Shima saw her chance to move in. Everything was about to change.

Shima honed in on Trisha who was dreaming she was packing luggage, and savoring a one-way ticket to the Caymans. The opportunity Shima needed to turn him against Trisha was about to manifest. She was convinced he would dump Trisha and choose her. Together they would take the money and travel the world leaving Trisha behind.

Shima closed her eyes and willed herself to find the man of her dreams. Though her heart was hard, her will was strong and it took only a moment of imagining his attributes before she was transported to an opportune place in the unraveling dream sequence.

*Pause, pause, pause...*

Amelia followed Jojo through the transporter beam to the kitchen of Miguel's house. Jojo opened the refrigerator door and peered inside. "I'm hungry," he announced.

"Jojo, we don't have time for food," Amelia whispered as if she was trying to hide from something. She peeked through the swinging door that separated the kitchen from the dining room and saw Miguel facing in her direction talking to a man seated at the table with his back toward her. Amelia wasn't sure whether she and Jojo were manifesting in Miguel's sleeping dream or the waking dream in which case Miguel might not be able to see her. She listened to the conversation in the dining room as Jojo heaped peanut butter and jelly onto two slices of bread and slapped them together.

"What about Lovelle?" the seated man asked Miguel. "Could he have been the shooter in the drive-by and the alley?"

"Possible." Miguel knew that Darius had been stalking Jojo. But he knew that Amelia did not recognize the driver even though she had seen Darius briefly on the mountainside. *Still*, he thought, *accuracy is not a feature of severe trauma.*

"Maybe Darius is behind all of this," Nick suggested.

*No*, Amelia thought, *it's Trisha*. She was about to burst through the door into the dining room to tell Miguel about seeing David in the Wait Zone. The man stood up and started to turn toward the door. Amelia was frozen in place. She couldn't move even to let the door close a little more. His eyes were darting around the room and missed Amelia.

*It's him*, she thought, as she studied the face of the man she had seen through the open window of the Camaro as it passed by Miguel's house. *How can Miguel be talking to HIM?*

"Miss Amelia?" Jojo whispered.

"Not now, Jojo," Amelia whispered holding her finger to her lips. Listening, she heard the man suggest to Miguel that they should go check out Darius and see what he was up to.

*No.* Amelia wished Miguel would hear her. *It's a trap. He knows damn well Darius didn't shoot at the house and he probably shot*

*David too.* Her observations simultaneously fit and failed to make sense. *But how does he know Miguel?*

Amelia watched as Miguel rose from his seat and grabbed his holstered pistol from the top of the buffet chest on the wall. She couldn't tell if the man had a gun with him or not. She looked down at her feet. The gold lamé shoes were in place. She was clearly not asleep and in their dream.

Amelia ran through the possibilities. *It is possible to be killed in the dreamtime if one believes his circumstances capable of ending his life -- unless a stronger dream intervenes.*

"Miss Amelia," Jojo tried again.

"Jojo, I'm *thinking*." Amelia hissed, turning to look at Jojo who was holding his peanut butter and jelly sandwich in mid air. Behind him was the unexpected presence of Shima who had joined them in the kitchen.

"Shima?" Amelia mouthed the name. "What are you doing here?"

"Taking care of business." Shima smiled darkly.

"Do you know who that guy is?" Amelia asked unsure of what was going on.

"Yes," Shima teased Amelia by filling in with no additional information.

"We have to stop him before he hurts Miguel." Amelia raised her hand toward the door.

From behind Jojo's back, Shima raised her hand holding the gun she had been pointing at him. Shima trained the gun on Amelia.

"What are you doing?" Amelia asked in disbelief.

"Getting what I deserve."

Amelia tried to conceive of what Shima meant and how she had managed to find her way into Miguel's dream. *How does she know how to do this?* Amelia wondered.

"You're not so special, Amelia," Shima smiled.

"You can hear my thoughts?" Amelia asked.

"Easily. You're so transparent," Shima replied.

"That guy out there shot me. Don't you care?" Amelia struggled to understand her adopted sister's cold stance.

"It wasn't my doing." Shima maintained her disinterested attitude.

Amelia felt confused even as she was becoming thoroughly convinced Shima had been part of dealing drugs with David and Trisha.

"You got in the way of something you don't understand at all." Shima smirked at Amelia.

Amelia countered, "Are you sure you understand? Because he went after David last night." Unlike Trisha, Amelia didn't imagine Shima would be supportive of violence against David.

Shima's hand holding the gun, dropped from its direct aim at Amelia. "He did not," Shima argued. Amelia knew she had struck a nerve.

"Yes, Shima." Amelia wondered at the way her eyes brimmed again with tears for her cheating ex-boyfriend. "Last night he killed David. Was it drugs?" Amelia blurted.

"Shut up!" Shima retorted. Amelia was surprised at Shima's apparent denial.

"I know David was involved with Trisha and they were making lots of money selling drugs!" Amelia declared.

Shima laughed a cackling sound and shook Jojo's shoulder as she demonstrated just how ridiculous something Amelia said seemed to her. "You don't know anything."

Amelia's mind jumped again to the money she'd seen in the suitcase at David's apartment. Shima tuned in to Amelia's thoughts.

"You were in on this?" Amelia stammered, "You helped take my money to buy and sell drugs?"

"Would you get over the drug thing?" Shima cursed with her tone. "What makes you think we were running drugs?"

"What else could have been in those packages Jojo was receiving for Darius Lovelle?"

"We did far better than selling drugs."

"What, then!  What the hell could you do that would generate that kind of cash?" Amelia demanded.

Shima smiled at Amelia's smug nature revealed.  *Of course, Shima thought to Amelia, you would never expect me to be capable of being part of such a grand plan.*

Amelia felt the shame of her less than admirable attitude toward Shima.  Beneath it all, she had plenty of resentments toward Shima.  She could never understand why her father had brought home a second daughter.  It was so strange to be usurped by suddenly receiving an older sister.

"Isn't that why you awarded me the manager job at Des Shoe?" Shima asked.  "Did it make you feel better to make me an employee?"  Amelia pressed her emotions to the back of her being and held her ground.

"It doesn't matter what I thought!  How were you able to make so much money if not by illegal means?"

"Oh, I didn't say it wasn't illegal.  I just said it wasn't drugs." Shima laughed inside her mind.  Amelia felt small and stupid.  "Secrets, Amelia."  Shima's words seemed to have a double meaning.  "Your dirty little secrets."

There was a commotion in the entryway.  They listened as Miguel introduced Nick to Alicia and explained to her that he'd be back in a few hours.  As Amelia watched Alicia climb the stairs to check on Jojo, she reached to push through the swinging door.

"Leave it," Shima ordered pointing the gun at Jojo to underline the importance of Amelia's compliance.

"What do you want me to do?"  Amelia pulled back from the door.

"Come with me."

"Where are they going?"  Amelia was filled with fear that at any moment she might hear a gunshot either inside or outside the house.

"To Darius Lovelle's house," Shima provided the destination.

"Darius?" Jojo whispered. By the power of Jojo's intimate knowledge of the place and two imaginings over one, the threesome was instantly transported to Jojo's bedroom in Darius' apartment.

*Pause, pause, pause...*

# 9

## *A Brain, a Heart...the Nerve!*

Darius Lovelle was considered by most to be a druggie who paid for his habit by performing random acts of stupidity. The last time Darius was busted by Nick, he was given the option of doing a little grunt work or being arrested. Darius opted for doing the cop's dirty work rather than spending time at the county jail.

Shima and Amelia listened to Darius as he thought his plan through while he was shaving.

*I should have never sent that boy,* Darius hissed in his own head. *Thought he'd a known he get a beatin' for messin' up that deal.* Amelia winced. *Stupid teacher.* Amelia knew he was thinking of her mom and how she called 241-KIDS to report the bruises Jojo couldn't hide.

"But I got it all under control." Darius stopped shaving and looked at himself in the mirror. "I'm goin' ta' get them first." He nodded to himself.

189

When Jojo failed to bring home the last package, Darius knew he had become a potential liability to the operation. When an anonymous source posted bond after Darius was jailed for hitting Jojo, Darius figured it was only a matter of time before someone laid him to rest.

In the days since his emancipation, he had quietly traced his contact's movements back to a house in the upscale part of town. Darius figured the operation had amassed hundreds of thousands of dollars from the deliveries he had assisted.

"And I ain't goin' through the regular channels ta' get what's mine." Darius dried his face with a towel, grabbed his jacket and left through the front door.

Miguel and Nick arrived in Miguel's Hyundai at the front of Darius Lovelle's apartment building just as he was hopping down the front steps toward the street.

Held at gunpoint, Amelia and Jojo watched from Jojo's bedroom window along with Shima. Miguel and Nick waited a moment after Darius pulled away from the curb in his old red Chevy Nova, and followed him into light traffic.

"Where are they going?" Amelia asked.

"Trisha's. Where else?" Shima replied.

That quickly the loathing that both Shima and Amelia felt for Trisha drove them along with Jojo through the ethers continuing in the style of a transporter beam from Jojo's snailing sequence.

"They'll be here in a minute," Shima predicted of Miguel and Nick as she stood beside Amelia in the driveway behind Trisha's house.

"Look! A pool!" Jojo looked at the large in-ground pool in Trisha's backyard. Instantly his clothes faded into swim shorts and Jojo took off running across the lawn.

"Help me out here." Amelia put her hand on her hip and turned to Shima. Her mind was filled with confusing questions.

"What part do you still not get?" Shima asked in a tone that indicated her patience was running short. Amelia shook her head. Despite the gun and betrayal she was surprised to find she still regarded Shima as a sister.

"Why is it that sometimes we can see each other and sometimes we can't? Who's dreaming and who's awake here?"

"It's four-thirty in the morning, Amelia." Shima sighed. "Everyone is asleep."

"Even you?"

"Some of us are lucid, some are not. Some are vibrating at the same frequency, others are off a bit." She looked at Jojo. "Even in waking life a child that age doesn't vibe in harmony with adults. So he can just go off and do his thing and most adults will never notice him even if they're in the same dream."

"So... I'm lucid?" Amelia asked.

"Not as much as I am," Shima insisted.

"How did you get so good at this?"

"I've been practicing since before I came to America." Shima seemed proud.

"It's a lovely way to leave behind what's too difficult to bear. Just like the boy over there." Amelia had a hard time reconciling Shima in a position to identify with Jojo. She saw Shima as undeservedly blessed given the way she had always behaved. She returned her attention to trying to figure out how each person was dreaming.

"And Miguel?"

"What about Miguel?" Shima's disinterest in Miguel was obvious via the tone of her voice.

"How is he dreaming?"

"Lucid. But not aware of our presence."

"What about Darius?"

"Dreaming." She paused. "He has wild dreams. And since Miguel and Nick are dreaming involvement with him, they are able to follow and interact with him."

"Is Nick," at last Amelia had a name for her shooter, "is he lucid?" Amelia asked.

"Not yet, but he'll wake up soon. Miguel dreamed him up this morning. Though he had been following you around in your dreams the past couple days."

"Really?" Amelia asked, "Nick was following me? You said he wasn't supposed to shoot me."

"He wasn't. He was supposed to take out Miguel, but he couldn't do it, especially when he saw him on the porch with a kid. That was their mutual soft spot — kids." Shima's eyes dazed slightly. "So he just shot wildly at the house until he could come up with another solution. But you got in the way."

"How do Nick and Miguel know each other?" Amelia still didn't understand the connection.

"Cops. They were cops together."

"Nick was a *cop*?"

"Still is. And your interest in finding out who he was drew his detective senses to you on the other side. He thought you might have seen him at the house. He couldn't let you send him to prison. Cops can't survive in prison."

"But I don't remember him trying to hurt me anywhere in my dreams."

"Never got a chance, just the sight of Miguel always stopped him. Nick's really a good guy at heart." Shima finished.

"Yeah, he seems really nice," Amelia toned sarcastically, "but he shot David."

Shima's body registered immediate tension. "I don't know why you keep saying that. It can't be."

Amelia tried to understand Shima's denial over David's demise. Zeroing in on Shima's thoughts, words were not forthcoming. Instead she felt jealousy toward her relationship with David, and a sense of competition. *You wanted David?!* Amelia screamed in her head. *Trisha wanted David?* Shima spun on her heel and stared at Amelia.

"What the hell is so great about David?" Amelia nearly shouted out loud, then felt herself splashed as Jojo ran up and stopped beside her.

"You ought to come to the pool!" Jojo dripped water onto the blacktop watching Amelia and Shima stare at each other while Trisha loaded luggage into her car.

"Why's she going on vacation?" Jojo commented on Trisha's activity. "She's got a pool right here!" He ran back across the pavement to the pool.

"And her?" Amelia nodded at Trisha struggling with the largest bag. "Is she lucid?" Amelia asked.

"Totally asleep."

"So, what's the point?" Amelia asked Shima. "Why are we here?"

"You'll see." Shima nodded toward the front of the house. Amelia looked up to see Darius sneaking through the bushes on the side of the house, toward the backyard. She watched in utter amazement as he skulked toward them without noticing them at all. Pleased to see he was invisible to Darius, Jojo started dancing around him making faces and sticking out his tongue. Darius remained completely oblivious to Jojo, as his eyes were totally fixed on Trisha.

As Trisha struggled to land a large suitcase in the back of her Acura SUV, Darius imagined it was full of money. Amelia watched as he suddenly reversed his attention and retraced his steps back toward the street. Trisha was leaving. As Darius opened the door to his Nova, Amelia looked past him and saw that Miguel and Nick were parked on a cross street with a clear view of his activities.

*Pause, pause, pause...*

"What's he doing?" Nick sounded slightly panicked as he watched Darius cross the street.

"Not sure." The tone in Nick's voice reflected his own senses.

He watched Darius return from behind the upscale brick house, get in the Nova, and slide down in the seat peeking over the dashboard. *What the heck brings someone like Lovelle to a neighborhood like this?* Miguel wondered.

A moment later Trisha's silver Acura started backing out of the driveway. She didn't see the Hyundai or the Nova waiting for her to lead the way as if she was at the head of a parade. In quick succession, Darius pulled down the concrete-paved street following Trisha, while Miguel and Nick followed not far behind.

"Now what?" Amelia asked Shima as they watched the three cars depart.

"Now we head to the airport," Shima replied. No transporter beam visual effects went off. No one moved or faded from view.

"Oh we do?" Realizing the compliance of her imagination was required to make the transition, Amelia felt empowered. By the look in Shima's eyes, she was.

"It's your choice." Shima threatened Amelia. "Either you go with me or you won't be able to help your Miguel if Nick decides to get rid of him."

*My Miguel.* Amelia repeated internally. She recognized the feelings that had started to grow for him in Main Street America had grown into fierce loyalty and a sense of protection, if not other more delicate feelings. She hated that Shima could tell.

"Ah, it's so cute." Shima felt mildly nauseous over the sweetness of Amelia's sentiments for Miguel.

"I'll go," Amelia reciprocated, "if you'll tell me what you did to get the money."

"Oh, the drug money? Try the remote line through your home computer." Shima dangled the information in front of Amelia and waited for her to catch on.

Amelia drew a blank. "I don't get it."

"That's what made it all so easy." Shima smiled, obviously enjoying the confusion she was causing Amelia. "Your files. David accessed your client files from your home computer."

"For what?"

"Information." Shima stomped her foot impatiently. "Saleable information." Amelia looked dumbstruck.

"Am I to understand that you sold my client's corporate secrets?" Amelia's mind pieced together the lawsuits, and lost court cases that had become a growing problem for her clients, "To their competition?"

"Competition, consumer groups, politicians, anyone who would pay." Shima dully studied the slew of connected thoughts that flooded Amelia's mind.

"Trisha was behind this?"

"Indeed."

"*How* did Nick get involved?" Amelia still didn't understand how Miguel was hanging out with a criminal cop.

"He had access to losers like Darius who could run the packages." Shima filled in another blank.

"How did she know him?" Amelia couldn't put together how a lawyer could con a cop into foul play.

"She did an internship at the station." Shima rolled her eyes as she grew bored. "She just knew him okay?"

"And you? How did you get involved?" Amelia couldn't believe her own sister had been a willing accomplice in a plot that would land her in the hospital with multiple gunshot wounds.

"*Adopted* sister," Shima corrected. "That's all you've ever thought of me."

"Well you *are* my adopted sister!" Amelia shouted thinking how much easier her life would have been as a child and at this very moment, if her father had never found Shima.

"That's what you thought," Shima hissed, "but he was my father too. My real father!" The words stunned Amelia.

"Liar!" Amelia accused.

"Why would I lie about that?" Shima raised her hands with an air of exasperation. "Why would I want to be the hidden child? Hidden from you, from the world, from having full investment in the family. He lied to you, little sister. He cheated me and he cheated you."

Amelia felt the wall between her and Shima thicken. She wanted to strike out. Then she regained her composure and thought better of it. Amelia decided it would be better to win now and ask questions later.

"Now, you must go to the airport with me!" Shima ordered. With Amelia's compliance the transporter beam again ignited the threesome's passage to a new location.

Shima seemed to be able to transcend time and see what was going to happen before it actually took place. Amelia realized this was what made Shima more lucid than she was in this dream.

Amelia attempted to process the deluge of information while they were engulfed in the transporter beam where she imagined it would be more difficult for Shima to read her thoughts in the flux of time and space.

Without an agenda of her own Amelia realized she would remain subject to Shima's dream. Somehow, she needed to get Miguel's attention. She wasn't sure that this would be possible since Miguel wasn't expecting her. Equally as problematic was not making Nick lucid. She hoped that she could get to Miguel before Nick tried to finish her off.

*Pause, pause, pause...*

The silver Acura pulled into the parking lot for Hanger 22 at Skyward Airlines. Amelia, Shima and Jojo waited on the outskirts of the hangar as Darius pulled past the turnoff into the farmer's market parking lot. Miguel pulled the Hyundai up to a parking meter outside the small main terminal at Lunken Airport.

"Who do you figure is in that Acura?" Miguel asked Nick. He had long been aware that he was dreaming so hadn't bothered to contact headquarters for assistance.

Nick had noticed that Miguel seemed to be playing the investigation close to his vest, but had not ascertained why until he himself became lucid with the recognition of Trisha. Now his dream was turning into a nightmare as he realized she was in the process of leaving him holding a bag filled with a big, incriminating mess.

Nick had met Trisha when she was part of the law team for the division of internal affairs at the department. She had represented him when he was investigated for his involvement in the shooting death of a young woman named Tonya Lovelle. Nick had been found innocent of shooting the woman. She had died instantly when she was caught in gang crossfire.

Nick could feel his cheeks redden as he watched Trisha interacting with the baggage clerk in the hangar. He felt abandoned as he had when Miguel pursued his own career and left him humiliated by desk duty. Trisha seemed to understand him then. When she laid out her plan for Nick it looked like a win/win situation with no one losing but big corporations and Trisha's lawyer boss. Nick admired his new partner in crime as she easily swayed David to retrieve the information from Amelia's private files. He justified what was essentially a bid for attention on his part, by putting his share of the take in a fund for Tonya Lovelle's son.

Nick had enlisted Darius as a runner and put his trafficking skills to use with materials less likely to get him shot than drugs. He figured Darius would make good money and have the time he needed to raise Jojo. He had no idea Darius would become so lazy he would actually use the child to make the pick-ups. He never thought David would be dumb enough to start giving Jojo the information or that the boy would tell social services about the packages he was transporting.

In his wildest dreams, Nick definitely never thought he would shoot anyone by accident or deliberately. Everything had become incredibly complicated and shady compared to the Robin Hood feeling he had when it all started.

From the window of the Hyundai, Nick watched as Trisha opened the trunk of her SUV and the baggage handler began extracting the luggage. As he watched the man drop the big suitcase onto the dolly he grabbed the door handle and sprang from the car.

"Nick!" Miguel yelled as he got out of the car and started following his ex-partner across the tarmac. The call caught Darius' attention and he too got out of his car and bolted for the baggage dolly at Hangar 22. Trisha heard the yelling and went lucid as her dream collided with the dreams of the three men heading toward her down the runway.

Trisha grabbed her purse from the front seat of the Acura and turned to leave the hangar but came face to face with Amelia and Jojo being held at gunpoint by Shima. The three men ran to a stop within a few yards of the three women and the boy.

"What the hell?" The baggage handler stared at the strange group that had assembled in what had just a few minutes earlier been an ordinary work dream.

Shima motioned with the gun and ordered the baggage handler, Amelia, and Jojo to join Miguel inside the hangar. Her business now was with Trisha, Darius and Nick.

"Trisha, what are you doing?" Nick implored.

"She's leavin' asshole," Darius sniped at Nick and looked at Shima. "Why don't we take this bag from the bitch and split it up between us?"

"Now why would I agree to do that? I am the one holding the gun," Shima challenged. "I get the money."

"The hell you do!" Trisha glared at Shima. "You all think I'm stupid enough to carry cash?" Silence prevailed among the foursome.

"Give it to me." Shima's eyes were locked on Trisha's purse as she realized the key to the money must be inside it. Trisha tossed her head and laughed.

"You have no choice." Shima pushed the barrel of the gun in

Trisha's direction, and brought her laughter to a stop.

Trisha looked at the lump under Nick's left arm. Seeing that he was armed, she decided to play into his loyalty. "Baby, I was just about to call you," she cooed. "I knew that Shima was up to something and you weren't home, so I came here. I was going to call you and tell you to meet me."

"Liar!" Shima stopped her story. "Nick." He turned to Shima. "Ask to see the tickets. There's only one."

"How do you know?" Nick asked, not trusting either one of them.

"Ask the baggage guy," Shima challenged, "he knows how many were flying."

The baggage handler stared at Shima in horror as Nick drew his gun and pointed it at the man. "Why me?" he asked. "Can't you just leave me out of this?"

Amelia barely noticed the baggage handler stepping to hide behind her as she tried to reconcile the conflicting evidence that was being presented. Despite the fact that she was a possible target for yet another bullet, what caught her attention most was Trisha's apparent intimate relationship with Nick as well as David.

"You are beein' reedicoollust!" Darius interrupted waving his arms.

Nick spun around, and pointed the gun at him.

"Listen man," Darius put his hands up and tried to calm Nick down. "You can't believe either one of these chicks. They're both lyin' to you!"

"So who should I believe, Darius? You?" Nick was becoming lost in his own rage. "I've been trying to help you for years and the thanks I get is finding you sneaking up here behind my back just like these two, trying to beat me to the chase." Nick wheeled at the realization he had become dependent on the likes of Darius Lovelle for help.

"I lost my cell phone, man." Darius tried to cover. "You know I got your back!"

"Oh, God, Nick!" Shima broke into a voice that showed her feelings for him. He spun around again and pointed the gun at her. "I wasn't trying to get the money. At least not take it away from you. I wanted it *and* you. I just let you come this far so you could see that she was not being real with you. I am being real with you Nick. We can take that money and leave right now."

"What are you talking about woman?" Nick's face flared with blood vessels popping through reddening skin. "We can't go anywhere! Look around you! Any single one of these people could put us in jail for life. You're crazy Shima! It's over."

"But Nick, I love you!" Shima cried.

"You don't know what the hell love is!" Nick shouted back at her.

"But I know you! I know you're good. You didn't mean to hurt Amelia and I know you didn't hurt David." Shima read Amelia's memory of the black Camaro leaving the Alley. "Tell her Nick. Tell her it was Trisha who shot him." Amelia felt completely confused as both Trisha and Shima focused all their interest on Nick not seeming to feel any remorse for the passing of David.

"Wrong again." Nick dropped his hand to his side letting the gun point at the ground as he acknowledged what he had done.

Miguel's police instinct kicked in and his hand immediately moved to his own holstered pistol.

"NO!" Shima shouted as she turned the gun on Miguel and squeezed the trigger. The bullet caught Miguel in the shoulder and threw him to the ground. Amelia dropped beside him, grabbed Miguel's face in her hands and looked deeply into his eyes.

"You're not going anywhere," she insisted. Amelia looked down and pressed her hand against the growing blood stain on Miguel's shirt. "My dream of you alive is bigger than her shot at you."

Miguel looked at Amelia remembering how he had gone to her bedside when she coded.

"I'm staying," he promised.

Jojo stared at Amelia leaning over Miguel. His eyes darted from his stepfather to Nick to Shima standing with the gun trained on Trisha. In a moment he was transported to a time almost before memory when his mother had fallen in front of him on the street outside their apartment building. His mind locked on his mother's face, his body was filled with rage and resolution. He wasn't going to let anyone else get hurt.

Jojo pounded his right hand to his upper left chest and imagined he hit the communicator button that connected him with the snailing vessel he believed was orbiting around the planet. "Sir Galahad!" Jojo shouted. Everyone's attention turned to the boy. "I need you to get down here.... NOW!"

Amelia watched as Shima focused her attention on the sky with Jojo. She knew Shima was seeing something that had not yet become apparent to her. Of course just about everything she thought had been apparent turned out not to be. So she just knelt on the ground next to Miguel and watched in rare silence.

An eerie sound filled the air not unlike that of Amelia's coffeemaker or more likely, twin turbo engines coming in for a landing. But nothing appeared to be coming down the landing strip. One by one the attention of each person standing on the tarmac was called upward. One by one each individual added to his or her dream the sight of a giant snail falling out of the sky, throttling toward them, underside first, at rocket speed.

In the amount of time it takes for an eight year old boy to blink his eyes, Sir Galahad landed squarely on top of Trisha, Shima, Nick and Darius leaving only their legs and arms visible as they stuck out from under his belly. Sir Galahad looked at the mangled mess of human extremities beneath his soft underside and curled his upper lip with an expression of disgust. His long tubular eyes stretched down to ogle Jojo.

"You rang?" he calmly checked in.

The luggage clerk looked at the mess of arms and legs extending out from under the talking snail. Amelia couldn't believe what she heard next. "They're dead!" the baggage handler exclaimed in a Munchkinland voice. He looked at Amelia, Miguel and Jojo. "You've killed them!"

*Whirl, whirl, whirl...*

For a moment Amelia felt as if she was caught up in some grand reversal of the tornado scene that had delivered the house atop the wicked witch of the east. All of the scenery faded and blurred. Miguel and Jojo went sailing past her peripheral vision. She thought she saw Shima fly by on a bicycle, followed closely by Trisha riding a broom and donning a deep green tint to her skin. She heard arguing and awakened to find she was standing with Jojo and Miguel while Shima, Trisha, Darius and Nick stood by and watched speechlessly as Hrim, Jahni and Tetta scolded the huge snail that had landed on them.

"You're not allowed to interfere!" Jahni threw up his hands in the air and turned around in circles. "What are we going to do?"

"I didn't interfere!" Sir Galahad defended himself. "Jojo called and I answered."

"You smooshed four people to death!" Hrim pointed up the long tall neck of Sir Galahad as his long eye tubules bent down to see him.

"It's not my fault the transporter beam can't support the weight of a ten ton snail!"

"Dumbo!" Jojo shouted gleefully and ran toward the snail smiling from ear to ear. "You did it, you're my hero!"

"Not now kid." The snail muttered out of one side of his mouth. "I'm having a little trouble here."

"Tetta," Amelia appealed to her one-time guru, "I know this probably is a little out of line, but isn't it true that Sir Galahad isn't exactly responsible for their deaths?" Tetta considered it was actually the belief of the victims that had brought them to their demise within the context of their own dreams. In thought she weighed in with the other guides to see if it was necessary for her to provide this information to the recently departed. In a moment she turned to the foursome.

"You all have been killed off in your dreams. If any one of you knows of someone who would have a stronger dream that you might remain alive, speak now or forever hold your peace."

Trisha looked at Nick and hung her head knowing he would not dream her back to life. Shima looked at Nick and knew she never got a chance to share such a dream with anyone in her life. "Nick," Shima offered, "I can dream you back to life."

"To spend it in prison?" He looked at Miguel. "I don't think so." His attention fell to Darius who was strangely quiet. His eyes were fixed on the radiant glowing figure of a woman standing a few yards away. Nick recognized the light-flooded face of Tonya Lovelle as she gazed upon Darius. Slowly Darius began to slump to the ground until he fell to his knees.

"I'm sorry." Darius broke down. "I-I'm so sorry. I've been terrible. I let you down. I hurt your son. I've missed you so much, Tonya."

The glowing woman smiled at Darius and Nick. Tears stung at the edges of Nick's eyes. Inside his head he heard the soft voice of a young woman.

*You tried too. Now you must forgive yourself.* Nick fell to his knees like Darius. The woman turned to Jojo and held out her arms bending low to the ground. Trisha and Shima looked at each other with the jealousy of jilted lovers.

"Momma!" Jojo ran to his mother and buried his face in her long hair. Miguel and Amelia looked on in amazement as Jojo reunited with his mom.

"In the Wait Zone," Hrim explained to Miguel and Amelia, "there are victims' rights. When those who have harmed someone arrive in the Wait Zone, their victim may greet them. Tonya has the final say on certain issues. She is forgiving Darius and Nick even though

203

neither of them has been able to forgive themselves for their shortcomings."

Tonya looked up at Miguel and Amelia as she placed her hands on Jojo's shoulders, and kneeled down in front of him to size him up. "You have turned into such a fine young man," she whispered lovingly. "I have always kept an eye on you, baby."

"You have?" Jojo's eyes widened in the light radiating from his mother.

"Yes, and I would really like to see you improve that math grade." Jojo's expression went bashful as he turned to Miguel and Amelia. "Did you hear that? She wants me to do my homework."

"You have been very good to my son." She smiled at Miguel and Amelia. "I am asking that you continue to care for him as his father will be staying here now."

Miguel nodded and Amelia felt a tear come to her eye as Tonya pulled Jojo toward her and hugged him close.

Jahni tilted his head forward as if he had been downloading information from the Akashic. He looked up at the giant snail and ordered Galahad to disembark the shell. Slowly the snail began to shrink. As it plummeted toward its original smaller than half dollar size, a lanky, middle-aged man with dark, slicked back hair, a five o'clock shadow and a cigarette in his mouth was revealed. None of the dreamers had ever seen him before. Despite his less than angelic appearance, he was wearing a white robe and sandals similar to Hrim and Jahni's.

"Used to be an off-Broadway director," Hrim commented to Miguel. "He still thinks he can make up his own ending."

"You are now responsible for mediating the karmic outcomes between these four," Jahni motioned with his left hand, "and this one." Trisha, Shima, Nick and Darius audibly groaned as David stepped out of the shadows of the Wait Zone.

"It's all your fault." Shima glared at Trisha.

"Your fault," Trisha argued.

"It was your brilliant plan," Nick sided with Shima.

"It's ev'rybody's fault that we gotta' keep on dealin' with Pretty Boy here," Darius nodded at David.

"Do I have to?" Galahad whined to Jahni and Hrim.

"That should keep you busy for centuries." Hrim nodded emphatically. Galahad started to usher his new assignments toward the orientation room as they continued to argue.

"Hi. My name is David." David tried to introduce himself to Nick. "And you are?" Everyone groaned in unison.

"Wait!" Amelia called out. She turned to Tetta. "Can I dream Shima back to life?"

"Don't do me any favors." Shima sharply cut at Amelia.

"But..."

"Nothing. You can't make up for it Amelia. Your dream really isn't stronger than mine. When you gonna learn that?" Despite her words Shima's eyes glistened with tears of gratitude that Amelia would consider trying to help her at all.

"It isn't fair." Amelia argued. Looking at Shima in the Wait Zone she saw the truth of her father's deathbed confession and felt the shame of his need to keep Shima secret even as he tried to honor her murdered mother. As she tapped into this truth another woman appeared on the scene. The resemblance was undeniable.

Amelia watched as Shima recognized her mother and became uncharacteristically vulnerable and innocent. Shima looked back at Amelia as she placed her hand in her mother's hand. Behind Amelia stood their father. Shima waved to him and Amelia, unaware of his presence, waved gently in return, as Shima and the others disappeared from sight.

Hrim bent low, picked up the snail from the misty cobblestones, and joined Amelia and Miguel. "Your wound is just superficial dream stuff," he said to Miguel. "There will be no physical evidence."

Hrim walked over to Jojo and Tonya Lovelle and waited while they completed their conversation.

205

"Do you live in heaven, Momma?" Jojo's eyes reflected the radiance of her figure.

"Well, now I guess that depends on what you believe." Tonya smiled. "If you think heaven is a destination where you just lay around and do nothing forever, then no, I do not live in heaven."

Jojo frowned as he had always pictured his mother wearing wings and playing a harp while sitting on a cloud. Tonya tipped her head low and caught his eye.

"But, if you believe heaven is a way to learn about living and grow to become a better person, then I definitely am in heaven most of the time." Jojo bounced on his feet nodding his understanding. "And you can be in heaven most of the time too young man, when you are committed to do the same everyday."

"I will Momma. I am!" Jojo threw his arms around his mother's shoulders and she hoisted him up as she stood and turned to Hrim.

Jojo dropped to the ground and accepted Dumbo as Hrim handed him the snail. "Take good care of that," she smiled, "and don't forget, your momma loves you very much." Jojo watched as his mother spoke quietly with Hrim for a moment, waved, and faded from sight.

"I want straight A's this year!" Tonya Lovelle's voice whispered in a fading tone.

Jahni and Tetta joined Hrim and led Jojo back to Amelia and Miguel. Jahni shook Amelia's hand. "It's been a lovely project, really, I hope to see you at University. I think we'll be able to get you some life credits for this experience."

"University? Life credits?" Amelia looked at Hrim and Tetta.

Hrim laughed and winked at Amelia.

"I'll explain it all next time I see you," Tetta reassured Amelia.

"Can you tell me just one thing?" Amelia begged Hrim to scan the Akashic for her.

"I'll do my best." He nodded once.

"So..." Amelia stammered, "David and Trisha?"

"Nope, just business."

"And Shima, she didn't either?"

"Nope, just Nick." Hrim didn't even have to scan.

"But who was the SHE that David kept referring to?" Amelia begged to know who David declared his undying love for just before he died.

"The *store*, dear." Tetta leaned forward and whispered to Amelia, "Perhaps you should take that as a hint, dear, and maybe look for a man who truly loves *you*, not just your shoes." She nodded at Miguel. Amelia blushed and glanced down at the gold lamé shoes. She had grown accustomed to them. She looked up expectantly.

Hrim acknowledged the sign that their business was finished. He looked at his wrist as a watch appeared. He turned his head and nodded at Tetta. The guides took a step back as Amelia, Miguel, and Jojo instinctively joined hands.

"Repeat after me." Hrim smiled curiously at Amelia. "There's no place like home!"

## Discussion Points
*(There just happen to be nine. They are not organized by chapter.)*

1. Zeke explains to Amelia that he knows the dream they're experiencing is hers because he doesn't have an accent in his own dreams. How can this compare with how we relate to others in our day-to-day life?

2. During the moon lesson, Tetta teaches that it is the human form that creates the illusion of "other" and "duality". How is her explanation of how consciousness works different and similar to Zeke's lesson on dreams?

3. How could Hrim's philosophy of right and wrong taught at the university, improve the condition of our daily life?

4. When Tetta is asked if she is something "other than" human she talks about the illusion of duality and how it affects human life. How is duality used by humans to produce both positive and negative experiences?

5. When Jojo has a traumatic experience with the clown, his imagination produces a unique hiding place. His imagination also puts him in some precarious situations as on the mountain trail. What could we teach Jojo to strengthen this ability for good rather than be only the affect of living in a traumatic environment?

6. The Law of Attraction says we attract what we focus our attention upon. How does Miguel's experience in the coffee shop with the spoon in particular, relate to how this idea does and sometimes doesn't seem to work?

7. Lucid dreaming is explained as awareness that a dream is occurring. Several characters in the book posit the idea that everything is a dream. How might lucid dreaming work in daily "waking" life?

8. At varying levels of consciousness certain characters are visible or invisible to others. What are your thoughts on this multi-dimensional existence? Is it real or imagined?

9. Various characters have differing opinions of what heaven and hell are all about. Whose ideas have you shared at some point in your life and with whose are you most closely associated with at this point in time?

About the Author

Pic Michel is an artist and writer living with her family in Cincinnati, Ohio. Pic conducts workshops to facilitate professional and life-skill development of the creative process for adults and children. Her interest in the practical application of the spiritual, quantum physical, psychological aspects of life permeate her writing, paintings, and workshops. More may be learned by visiting her website at www.cpicmichel.com

www.ingramcontent.com/pod-product-compliance
Lightning Source LLC
Chambersburg PA
CBHW070116260626
47160CB00004B/1500